Praise for
THE THROWBACK SPECIAL

"Wistful and elegantly written. . . . [I]ts imaginative fresh-
ness allows for sly new questions to be implicitly asked
about men's relationship to sports, to violence, to nostalgia
and to one another. . . . *The Throwback Special* conjures the
rewarding melancholy of Richard Ford's Frank Bascombe
novels."   —John Williams, *New York Times Book Review*

"A gem. . . . Bachelder's 'football' novel is an eerie, witty
work dissecting a modern-day sacrificial (sack-rificial?)
ritual."   —Matt Seidel, *The Millions*

"[Bachelder] excels as an analyst of the anxieties that
undergird social mores."
                       —Miranda Popkey, *The New Yorker*

"Bachelder's quirky, defiant style . . . achieves something
fresh and surprising."
                    —Chris Tucker, *Dallas Morning News*

"[*The Throwback Special*] is not about football. But about
relationships and all that go with them: trust, mistrust,
joy, sadness, elation, heartbreak and more."
                    —Vic Fleming, *Memphis Daily News*

"[A] deeply satisfying brew of wry, sorrowful humor."
—Michael Kalisch, *Times Literary Supplement*

"Poignant and droll. . . . [T]here is absolutely something for everyone (even the sports-averse) in this rollicking, irreverent but sweet human drama."
—Julia Jenkins, *Shelf Awareness*

"With slow, magnifying prose, Bachelder pays equal attention to—and conflates—both the revelatory and the banal, and achieves a tremendous sense of life."
—Zack Hatfield, *Full Stop*

"What a terrific novel, even for non-football fans."
—Nancy Pearl, author of *Book Lust*

"A hilarious literary novel about our least hilarious—and least literary—national pastime. No one who reads it will ever be able to think about football, Joe Theismann, Lawrence Taylor, or indeed the male psyche in quite the same way again."
—Tom Bissell, author of *Apostle*

"A comic meditation about marriage, ritual, friendship, parenthood, aging, and unlikely obsessions. *The Throwback Special* is a funny, insightful, and surprisingly poignant book."
—Julie Schumacher, author of *Dear Committee Members*

THE
THROWBACK
SPECIAL

Also by **Chris Bachelder**

Abbott Awaits

U.S.!

Bear v. Shark

THE
THROWBACK
SPECIAL

A NOVEL

Chris Bachelder

W. W. NORTON & COMPANY
Independent Publishers Since 1923
NEW YORK · LONDON

Portions of this book appeared in a slightly different form in
The Paris Review.

For information about permission to reproduce selections from this book, write to Permissions, W. W. Norton & Company, Inc., 500 Fifth Avenue, New York, NY 10110

For information about special discounts for bulk purchases, please contact W. W. Norton Special Sales at specialsales@wwnorton.com or 800-233-4830

Manufacturing by Quad Graphics Fairfield
Book design by Fearn Cutler de Vicq
Production manager: Anna Oler

Library of Congress Cataloging-in-Publication Data

Bachelder, Chris.
The throwback special : a novel / Chris Bachelder. — First edition.
pages ; cm
ISBN 978-0-393-24946-0 (hardcover)
1. Male friendship—United States—Fiction. 2. Masculinity—Social aspects—United States—Fiction. 3. United States—Social life and customs—Fiction. I. Title.
PS3602.A34T48 2016
813'.6—dc23
                                    2015028394

ISBN 978-0-393-35378-5 pbk.

W. W. Norton & Company, Inc.
500 Fifth Avenue, New York, N.Y. 10110
www.wwnorton.com

W. W. Norton & Company Ltd.
15 Carlisle Street, London W1D 3BS

1 2 3 4 5 6 7 8 9 0

For Padgett Powell

and always for Jenn

What, then, is the attitude and mood prevailing at holy festivals?

—Johan Huizinga, *Homo Ludens*

THE
THROWBACK
SPECIAL

Today in Sports History

NOVEMBER 18, 1985 — WASHINGTON REDSKINS quarterback Joe Theismann, 36, suffers a career-ending compound fracture of the right leg on a sack by New York Giants linebacker Lawrence Taylor during a telecast of ABC's *Monday Night Football*. On first-and-ten from their own 46-yard line, early in the second quarter with the score tied 7–7, the Redskins attempt a trick play called a flea flicker. Theismann hands the ball off to tailback John Riggins, who takes several steps forward and then pitches the ball back to Theismann. Theismann looks to throw a deep pass, but he immediately faces pressure from Giants linebacker Harry Carson. "Theismann's in a lot of trouble," says play-by-play commentator Frank Gifford. He steps forward into the pocket to avoid Carson, but Taylor, rushing from Theismann's blind side, leaps onto his back. Theismann ducks, and as Taylor falls and spins, his thigh strikes Theismann in the calf with enough force to snap the bones of Theismann's leg. "It sounded like two muzzled gunshots," Theismann says later. Taylor stands quickly, waving to the Redskins sideline for medical help. ABC decides to show the reverse angle replay twice. "And I suggest," Gifford says before the replay, "if your stomach is weak, you just don't watch." "When you see a competitor like Joe Theismann injured, especially this severely, I don't think anyone feels good about it," commentator O. J. Simpson says. Theismann receives an ovation as he is carried from the field at RFK Stadium on a stretcher. "I just hope it's not his last play in football," says commentator Joe Namath. Jay Schroeder replaces Theismann at quarterback, and the Redskins defeat the Giants 23–21. Theismann, a former league MVP who had played in 163 consecutive games, never plays again.

- 1 -

THE ARRIVAL

"**W**OULD IT—"
The woman at the front desk was squinting disapprovingly at her monitor. She touched her temple with her fingertips, and blinked slowly, as if reluctant to resume eyesight. She did not look up.

"Is there any way that . . ."

The woman twisted her thumb ring, grimaced at the data on the screen. She was not, she made clear, available for hospitality. The thumb ring, purchased from a street vendor, was vaguely Celtic in design.

"Would it be possible, at all, to check in?"

Robert's voice was *too high*. He often had to remind himself to deepen his voice, but invariably it would rise again to a pitch that assured his auditor that he was nonthreatening. It was an animal signal; he might as well have had a shaggy tail tucked against his inseam. I submit to you, the pitch of his voice said. I acquiesce to the large desk, that brass pineapple. I would like another mint, but I will not take one. That clock behind me is immense, and though it appears to be slow, I will live by its decree.

"No," the woman at the front desk said, without looking up from her monitor. "I'm sorry," she added.

Robert nodded. "Thank you," he said in a voice so deep that it hurt his larynx. The woman vacated her position, indicating that the interaction was complete. Robert watched her as she walked into a secret room behind the front desk. Though a visitor, he felt abandoned.

Robert had been, characteristically, the first of the men to arrive at the hotel, a two-and-a-half-star chain off Interstate 95 recognized in online reviews for its exceptional service, atrocious service, pretty fountain, and bedbugs. He felt now the familiar burden of concern. It seemed, this and every year, profoundly unlikely that each of the other twenty-one men would show up. Standing alone by the fountain, holding a duffel bag and a football helmet, Robert had the anxious sensation that the ritual, seemingly so entrenched, was in fact precarious. He was dimly aware that his habit of arriving prematurely had more to do with apprehension than eagerness. He felt a need to count himself present.

The celebrated fountain in the center of the lobby was dry and quiet, cordoned off by yellow tape. A placard that partially obscured a notice from the department of health implored visitors to pardon the commitment to excellence. Scattered in the fountain's arid basin was a constellation of coins, whitish and crusted. Robert gripped the yellow tape, stared at the desiccated wishes.

There was nothing, he considered, more dry than an inoperative fountain.

Robert exited the lobby beneath an arbor of plastic vines. At the end of the hallway, the heavy door to the conference room was locked, but Robert peered through its small window. The carpet, a honeycomb design, was new, he thought. On the floor, propped against the lectern, was a framed poster of an icy summit that Robert could not recall from previous years. He tried the door again, but it was still locked. As he backed away, he nearly knocked over a wooden easel, which displayed, on a piece of creased foam board, the weekend schedule. The conference room, according to the schedule, was booked solid for a corporate retreat by a group called Prestige Vista Solutions. Robert double-checked the dates: November 17 and 18. Could he be, he wondered, in the wrong hotel? But no. There was the fountain, the huge clock, the weird brass pineapple. The dusty, waxen leaves of the arbor. He turned the foam board over, placing the schedule facedown against the easel. The reverse side displayed a bar code sticker and an inexpert pencil sketch of a dolphin.

Back in the lobby, Robert chose a stuffed chair in the corner where he could see anyone who arrived or departed. The day outside was raw and gray, the low clouds bulging with cold rain. Robert unsnapped the chinstrap from the helmet, and from his duffel bag he removed a sewing kit—a wicker box with a hinged lid—that had originally belonged to his first wife's aunt. In the kit he found a faded and lumpy pincushion originally made to resemble either a tomato or an apple or a strawberry. Robert selected a needle from the pincushion, then a spool of white thread from the tidy spool boxes in the kit. He threaded the needle, realizing as he did so that he had become someone for whom threading a needle is difficult. Robert began to mend the chinstrap, which had split longitudinally when he snapped it on last year. The white of the thread matched closely, though not exactly, the white of the chinstrap.

WHEN CHARLES PASSED THROUGH the automatic doors into the hotel lobby, he saw Robert sleeping in a chair so large and soft that it appeared to be slowly ingesting the unconscious man. Robert clutched a chinstrap to his chest like a rag doll. A small wicker box with a hinged lid sat overturned by Robert's feet, and a half dozen spools of thread, having emerged from the box, seemed to be making their perilous journey to the sea. Charles sat down on the edge of a soft chair, and Robert awoke, feeling embarrassed to be seen sleeping, then irritated for being made to feel embarrassed.

"Hello, Robert," Charles said.

"I tried to check in," Robert said, wiping the edges of his mouth with the collar of his shirt. He struggled to get out of the chair, reminding himself of his father. He knelt on the floor to pick up the errant spools of thread. Charles assisted by retrieving two spools, annoying Robert.

Charles asked Robert how his year had been.

"Not that great," Robert said. "What time is it?"

The wicker sewing kit reminded Charles of his grandparents' cabin on Lake Michigan. There had been a box there—though much larger, and not wicker—full of games and toys. While the adults talked and drank, he would sit on the floor, playing Barrel of Monkeys or Lincoln Logs. There had been another toy, a sketch of a bald man's head encased in transparent plastic. With a magnetic stylus you dragged dirty iron filings to the man's head, giving him hair, a mustache, a beard. The filings clung to the stylus like filthy moss. The man's mood was entirely dependent, Charles had discovered, on the angle of the eyebrows.

"Twelve forty-five," Charles said.

Robert tidied his sewing kit, and Charles regarded the chinstrap. Was it moths, he asked, that had damaged the strap?

"What?"

"Moths?"

"Not mine," Robert said. "Wesley's. Year before last."

"Wesley, yes," Charles said, with a scorn not linked to conviction. Wesley's gear was often musty. Both men idly remembered the year that Vince's Russ Grimm jersey ripped while he was pulling it over his shoulder pads.

"Where is everyone?" Robert said.

Charles, who counseled adolescent girls with eating disorders, wanted to tell Robert to put that thought in his worry box. "They'll be here," he said. "They always are."

Charles rose from his chair and walked through the lobby. He circled the dry fountain. The woman at the front desk did not look up from her monitor. The woman, like so many women, was formidably attractive to Charles, primarily because she was so unaware of him. A sense of his own insignificance often made him lustful. He gripped the yellow tape surrounding the fountain. The woman took a long strand of hair from the back of her head and pulled it over to the front. She stared at it cross-eyed for a moment, then yanked with grim determination. She frowned, dropped the hair to the carpet, stared at her screen. Her nudity was a fantastical premise, as speculative in its particulars as dark matter or quarks. Charles vaulted lust, arriving somehow in jealousy, which confused him. This seemed grounds for expulsion, and he left the lobby beneath the arbor of dusty vines. An easel outside the conference room door displayed a rudimentary sketch of a porpoise. He peered in, observed the new carpet, the burnished lectern. He returned briskly through the lobby to the sitting area, but did not sit.

Robert asked if Charles had seen the conference room schedule, and Charles shook his head.

"It's booked for a retreat," Robert said. "All weekend it's booked. Premium Vantage Systems or something." In Robert's imagination the retreatists all looked like sinister Bible salesmen. They just do whatever they want, Robert thought. They just despoil the environment and establish tax havens and seize conference rooms. They don't benefit society.

Charles stood looking out the window to the parking

lot. If it was not already raining, it would be soon. The sky had descended, gray and gravid. The automatic doors of the lobby opened, admitting only the wind, then closed.

"I wouldn't worry," Charles said. "We always have the conference room."

Gripping the mended chinstrap with both hands, Robert pressed it into his chin, testing its strength. His anger abated. It was difficult to sustain one's anger in a chair so large and soft. As it turned out, Robert needed to talk to Charles. There was something he had been worried about.

"I'm glad you're here, Charles," he said.

"Okay," Charles said, wishing he were still sleeping in a rest area.

"It's something that happened to my daughter."

"How old is she?"

Robert hesitated, wanting to get the answer right. "Six," he said.

Charles indicated that Robert should continue.

"Well," Robert said, "she broke her arm a couple of months ago on the playground."

Charles noticed all of the smudges on the glass of the plate window. It was a record of desire. People touch windows, he thought, for reassurance. Running counter to the narrative of expansion was an equally prominent narrative of containment. "Robert," he said, "you know I'm not a medical doctor. I'm a psychologist."

"I know. This isn't about her arm. Her arm healed up fine. It's somehow probably stronger now than it was before. Can you sit down?"

"I don't work with young children."

"No," Robert said. "This is more about me."

"I work with adolescents with eating disorders."

"The mind is the mind, right?"

Charles said that no, that was not right at all.

"When it happened," Robert said, "I was upset. When she broke her arm, I mean. I was upset."

"Sure. Of course."

"It was upsetting. Do not get me wrong. She fell off the monkey bars and landed on her elbow. I was standing right there. It wasn't like I was being inattentive. I was right there. Look, this would be easier for me if you were sitting down."

"It's not your fault, Robert. These things happen. Monkey bars, trampolines, bikes. When my son was—"

"She insisted on doing it. Absolutely insisted."

"So you feel guilty?" Charles asked. He felt both relieved and disappointed to have arrived at such conventional trouble. "Are you talking about feelings of guilt?"

"She was crying in a way that I could tell was not fake. She has a fake cry that makes me want to jump through a plate-glass window. Do you know that kind of fake cry I'm talking about?"

"Yes," Charles said. "I do."

"But this was real, I could tell. And I was upset. I wasn't glad about it."

"Why would you be?"

"Exactly," Robert said, laughing. "No. What?"

"Exactly," Charles said.

"It's not like I was happy when my own daughter broke her arm."

"Robert. The idea of normalcy in human thought is something of a controversial concept, but I can absolutely assure you that your response was normal."

"But still, I felt something weird. A twinge."

Charles closed his eyes, placed his forehead against the cool smudged glass. "A twinge?"

"A small one," Robert said, flailing for comfort in the enormous chair. With a calm voice Charles asked once again about the nature of the twinge.

"Not happiness!"

"What?"

"Not gladness," Robert said, pulling the chinstrap hard against his chin. "Maybe, I don't know, a kind of satisfaction?"

"Satisfaction at her broken arm?"

"Not satisfaction. Not that at all. Not satisfaction. Come on. She was really hurt. I felt terrible for her, and I was upset. She fell asleep in the car, Charles. Just passed out. Her body kind of shut down. I don't know, a certain kind of pleasure. But *not* pleasure. Maybe a twinge of vindication? It's hard to describe. Not joy. I wanted to talk to someone about it. That's why I was glad you came early."

"I always come early."

"This is a kid who just assumes everything is going to go exactly the way she wants it to go. She just knows everything works out. Maybe all kids are like this. Are all kids like this? She gets taken from the pool to the playground to the large inflatable climbing structures. She gets ice cream at all hours of the day. She has a thousand stuffed animals. We don't have a real pet, Charles, but the vacuum cleaner is clogged with hair. All day long I say No. No, no, no, but as I'm saying it, I'm reaching for my wallet."

Charles scanned the parking lot. Where was Tommy? Where was Gil? Where were Vince, Derek, and Steven?

"I drive her around looking for rainbows. We listen to princess music. Her booster seat has all these features. She hands me trash. 'Here,' she says, handing me fruit strips and chewed straws. I wipe food off her *forehead* and her *neck*, and I'm the bad guy, the mean dad. She has an idea about the way the world works, and this accident—falling off the monkey bars—was kind of a small—I don't know—corrective. I wasn't pleased, and I certainly never would have intentionally—"

"What?"

"—and I can't imagine I wouldn't have tried to catch her if I had been a step closer. But I did feel, for just a second, this awful sense of certainly not gladness but maybe *approval*. Because I thought that it would be a good lesson?—do you see, Charles?—about the way the world actually works. You know, *gravity*. The body. Force times velocity. There's not always some soft fairy bed of moss to—"

Charles said that he wanted to make sure that he understood clearly.

"I thought it might challenge her worldview," Robert said. "I don't know. I guess I just wanted to talk to someone about it. I wanted someone to tell me that it was normal for me to feel not glad, but you know, satisfied. Not satisfied."

Charles turned away from the window and sat in a chair across from Robert. He cleared his throat, leaned forward with his elbows on his knees. "Listen," he said. "What I do know about children is that it's important—some experts believe it is quite important—for children to negotiate risk and danger on their own, or else they might later be—or so it is thought—inordinately risk-averse and timid, too reliant upon parental intervention. Are you saying, Robert, that you felt satisfied that your daughter was negotiating risk in a developmentally healthy way?"

"Not exactly."

"Aren't you saying that, Robert? Isn't that the fairly normal thing you're saying?"

Robert said that it wasn't.

"Yes, it is," Charles said. "You're saying that, for your child's sake, for her own happiness and success, you would like her sense of reality to correspond more accurately to—"

"It was a different kind of twinge, Charles. It was like a twinge of justice. It was nearly the same feeling you get when you see very powerful people get indicted for corruption. When you see them duck into the backseat of a police car with handcuffs on. With the officer's hand on their head?"

Charles stood again, and returned to the window. He saw one of the Michaels—Fat Michael—get out of his car and stretch. The hem of his shirt slid up, exposing an inch of his toned and hairless abdomen. Fat Michael was in fact remarkably lean and muscular and well proportioned. His nickname was a typical masculine joke, a crude homemade weapon that indiscriminately sprayed hostility and insecurity in a 360-degree radius, targeting everyone within hearing range, including the speaker. Charles had shared the linebackers' hotel room (the "Fracture Compound") with Fat Michael two years ago, and he remembered that body with admiration and repulsion. Fat Michael's level of fitness made Fat Michael a walking rebuke of everyone else's lifestyle choices. He had those veins in his arms, and the kind of torso that tapers from chest to waist. He was a beautiful affront. He had engineered himself, his physical being, in his forties, to make others feel rotten, and what kind of person would do that? Without knowing it, Charles pinched the fat above his belt buckle. In the parking lot, Vince jogged over to Fat Michael—Charles thought Vince's strides seemed exaggerated—and the two men shook hands, then stared at the ground, talking, scuffing their shoes. Charles envied their inane pleasantries in the cold.

"Robert," he said, without turning around. Like certain zoo animals, the adolescents he worked with often did not want to be looked at directly. "When your daughter fell to the ground and then began crying in an authentic way, what did you do?" Charles knew this line of questioning was a substantial risk, but in his professional opinion it was justified. Also, he wanted this conversation to be finished.

Robert said that he got down on the ground with his daughter and brushed the wood chips out of her sweaty hair.

"I see," Charles said. "And did you hesitate?"

No, he did not hesitate. He tried to calm her down. He told her everything would be fine.

"And then what did you do?"

Robert said he asked his daughter if she could walk to the car, and she nodded. He said he told her she was a brave kid. He picked up the curtain sash that the child uses as her long imaginary braid. It had fallen off of her head. He dusted it off and tied it back around her head. Charles knew the curtain sash to be a warning sign, but he let it slide. Robert said he walked with his daughter for a while, and she was holding her arm completely still. She was trying not to cry. Her eyes were squeezed shut, and her lips were trembling. She was as white, Robert said, *as a sheet*. He said he carried her most of the way, as gently as he could. It was like carrying a horse. "You know," he said, "a baby horse."

"A foal, yes," Charles said, nodding. "And then?"

Robert said he called a doctor to get advice about where to take the child. Then he took her to an emergency care facility, where she got X-rays and a sling. The next day he took her to an orthopedist to get the cast.

"Yes," Charles said. "Right. Do you see? Do you hear yourself?" Charles said he saw nothing to worry about. Nothing whatsoever. He said, with a hot wave of self-reproach, that ultimately Robert was responsible for his actions, not his thoughts. Charles, though, had recently begun to suspect that people might not even be responsible for their actions.

"Thank you, Charles," Robert said, sinking farther into his chair. "I appreciate that."

But Robert had not gotten what he wanted. What had he wanted? How could it possibly be true that he was not responsible for his thoughts? If he wasn't, then who was? He rubbed his thumb across the velvety interior of the chinstrap. The orthopedist, the nurses—they had looked at Robert as if he were abusive. He had taken a child to the playground without a net, without elbow pads. And the cast! It was pink and purple with *glitter*. The girl got to choose the colors and patterns, even the toppings. She had been scared before the orthopedic appointment, and Robert sat on the edge of her bed and talked to her soothingly about how it would be fine, even fun, to have a cast. Everyone could sign her cast and draw pictures on it. He told her they could put a bread bag on it so she could take a bath. Pretty neat, right? Then the next day she gets this pastel waterproof Disney arm accessory, and she swims and bathes and doesn't let anyone else near the cast with a pen or marker. Girls on the street stare at her with that glazed envy that young girls stare at each other with. The cast glitter rains through the house, sparkling in nests of synthetic animal hair. Water flushes out the dead skin, so her arm doesn't get itchy at all. She never once has to ram a fork or chopstick into the cast to try to reach the agonizing itch. And when they cut the cast off? It really tickled, a lot. The girl had laughed and laughed. Then she got some stickers. She got to keep the cast as a souvenir. It didn't even smell bad. Robert took her out for ice cream with her curtain sash trailing down her back. She wanted to keep wearing the cast, so Robert taped the two pieces together with clear packing tape. Then he offered, for a reason he would never understand, to make a *neat bedside lamp* out of the cast. Would she like that? A lamp made from the cast? She answered affirmatively in a series of terrible, terrible baby noises.

Well, but at least he had not lied to her. He had told her the awful truth. He had said everything was going to be fine, and it was.

THE HOTEL PARKING LOT, in which there were no trees, was covered by a thick layer of leaves. The leaves had blown from afar to reach their final resting place. They decayed pungently in pulpy clumps the color of old pennies, impervious now to wind or leaf blower. Beneath this wet stratum of decomposing vegetative matter were the faded arrows, directing traffic flow circularly toward the check-in portico, primarily a nonfunctional architectural gesture of welcome, and only rarely utilized by Old World Europeans and those of very advanced age. The lot was divided by berms, mounded and sparsely coated with bark mulch and cigarette butts. Lights on poles defined the perimeter.

Power lines transected the airspace above the lot. There were few cars in the large lot, and all seemed to have been parked to maximize the distance between them.

The rain had begun, its inaugural drops fat and hostile. Vince and Fat Michael stood on a berm, staring upward with attitudes of appraisal and discernment. Vince's hand still ached from Fat Michael's handshake. Vince, whose grip was moderate, had attempted, mid-shake, to match Fat Michael's firmness, and consequently his greeting had been, he knew, restive and undisciplined. At what point, Vince had occasionally wondered, would daily life cease to consist of a series of small threats? What age must he achieve before the large cucumber was stripped of its dark power? Vince and Fat Michael were comparing forecasts for the weekend. Each, as it turned out, had a favorite meteorological website—chosen by chance and maintained by habit—and neither could quite accept the validity of rival predictions. Ignoring the real weather, they squared off about the conjectural weather. Vince scaled the berm to get taller. He suspected Fat Michael's site was dot-gov. Their forecasts were similar—rain was virtually certain—but each man might as well have been talking to the other about acupuncture or St. John's wort. Fat Michael rubbed his hands vigorously with antibacterial sanitizing gel.

Others by now had arrived. Tommy, Carl, Gil, Myron, Gary, Chad. Carl, in a galling violation of an unwritten but commonsense rule of the group, emerged from his extended cab pickup wearing his jersey from last year, that of Giants nose guard Jim Burt. As always, Gary drove in slow circles around the lot, blasting his horn and shouting community-sustaining threats and maledictions. A small school of men darted away from Gary's car, over two berms toward Derek's green sedan. After parking, Derek had lifted the hood, and he stood bent at the waist, peering down. Andy, sitting far away in his car with the engine still running, saw the men converge on Derek and his raised hood. The men spread out on the perimeter of the engine, gripping the edge of the car, like zealous spectators at a dice table. There was just enough room for everyone around the warm and possibly defective motor. Their duffel bags lay at their feet. Andy, who may or may not have been hiding here in his running car, turned on his wipers to watch them. They all stared down, nodding. Oh, pistons, oh, hoses! Derek was of mixed race, which is to say he was black. He was the only black man in the group, though Andy had noted that Derek's skin was a couple of shades lighter than the skin of Gil, the Floridian. So powerful was the allure of annual interracial acquaintance-ship that Derek almost always had a cluster of men around him, even in foul weather. And now this black man's car's hood was raised, creating an irresistible synergistic force, the dream of multiculturalism fused with the dream of automotive expertise. The rain was nasty now, cold and slant. Carl's Jim Burt jersey was obviously getting wet, forcing his cohorts to decide whether and to what extent Carl was an asshole. Other men arrived, and attended to Derek's engine: Jeff, Wesley, and Bald Michael, whose nickname, unlike Fat Michael's, was more or less accurate and nonironic, though still unkind. Andy watched as the engine summit drew to a close. Derek, always so resourceful, closed the hood and guided the men through the rain toward the protection of the check-in portico. They bowed their heads like monks. Gary, still driving the lot in festive, hostile circles, passed these men, honking and brandishing a shiny blue helmet through his sunroof. "Gentlemen," he yelled, "gird those puny loins!"

Andy turned off his wipers. He remained in his car with the engine running, pretending to inspect the bottom of his cleats. He held a shoe in one hand, and with the other he used a ballpoint pen to scrape at imaginary dirt around the studs. He had cleaned the cleats carefully earlier in the week, and of course he had cleaned them after the last time he had worn them, a year ago. They were very clean. He wasn't ready to go inside yet, and he was trying to give the impression to any possible witnesses that he was busy and content here alone in his parked and running car. Through the curtain of rain on his windshield he thought he saw George, the public librarian, doing calisthenics on a berm. George was someone Andy did not want to see. George's thin gray ponytail was just ridiculous, never more so than when trickling out of a football helmet. Whenever anyone asked George how he was doing or how his year had been, he always replied the same way: "Just doing my thing." Then he would talk, in a slow and agonizingly thoughtful way, about budget cuts at both the state and local levels, the power of information, the mar-

ketplace of ideas, the future of the book, the public's appe-
tite for memoir, the digital divide, and, worst of all, the
First Amendment. Andy hated talking to librarians, and
he did not want to be hugged. He cut his engine, not unlike
an animal playing dead. He worked earnestly and with
renewed vigor at the pretend mud in his cleats. A sudden
vaporous notion—he should not have come—dissipated
before it could condense into conviction. He kept his head
down, hoped George would menace someone else with his
idealistic interpretations of devastating factual evidence.

There was a tap on the passenger-side window. Andy
looked up to see George giving him what he believed to be
the first peace sign he had ever seen outside of documentary footage. George's face was so close to the window that
he was fogging the glass.

"Hi, George," Andy mumbled. He kept the doors shut,
the windows raised.

"Andy!" George said.

"How's it going?"

"Just doing my thing!" George yelled.

Andy pointed to his ear and shook his head, pretending
he could not hear. He hoped these conditions would prove
too difficult to support conversation.

"My thing!" George yelled.

Andy nodded.

"Our branch is closed on Tuesdays! Serious cuts!"

"Sorry to hear that," Andy said into his cleats. The rain
slid down the windshield and windows. Andy's anxious
breathing began to fog up the inside of the glass. George

became a wet and indistinct blur, but Andy could still hear him speaking slowly through the window. He was disappointed about a tax referendum in his county, but he still had faith in the democratic process. The information was out there. The people could find it, make informed choices. Then something about either wetlands or weapons. Andy remained silent, hidden in his fortress of condensation. He was not, at this point of the weekend, having a good time, though he knew that good times were probably just for teenagers dancing around a big bonfire in a clearing in the woods with loud music playing from an open hatchback. After a few minutes, the talking stopped and the foggy blur disappeared from Andy's passenger window. Andy had been inconsiderate, he knew. He thought of his wife, what she would say to him. She would say that he had been cruel to George. She would say that George wasn't so bad. She would say he's lonely. But Andy's wife was the person who invariably, at any social gathering, ended up cornered by a gesticulating freak. The eccentrics preyed on her, sensing her weakness, her gentle open face, her listening skills. They had things they wanted to share—their health problems, their pets' health problems, their unpublished fantasy novels, the fires that nearly destroyed their childhood homes, the recent spate of vandalism in their neighborhoods, their long estrangements from their felonious sons. Andy's wife would stand for hours with her back to the artwork, so careful not to touch it, clutching an empty glass of wine, making eye contact, nodding at the lunatic.

And then on the drive home she would brim with misanthropic rage. Why, she would want to know, had Andy not saved her? Could he not see that she was trapped by that woman with her fringed vest tucked into the elastic waist of her skirt? With those huge feather earrings? That woman talking for *over an hour* about chestnut blight? Andy recalled how strange it had been, in the first giddy months of marriage, to introduce her, to consider her, as his wife. And now it would be just as strange to think of her as his ex-wife.

Andy was startled by a loud knock on the driver's-side window. The blur outside the car looked like it might be George. It knocked again with knuckles, rubbed the window with the wet sleeve of its jacket. "Andy?" It was George. "Are you still in there? What are you doing?"

Andy considered this question. What was he doing? Was he doing his thing? Was hiding from librarians his thing?

"Can I come in?" George yelled.

Andy didn't answer. After a brief pause, George opened the back door, and got into the car behind Andy. Andy saw him in the rearview mirror. George was soaked, and dripping onto the cloth seats. He shivered and said, "Almost Indian summer weather here in mid-November," imitating Frank Gifford's commentary in the seconds before the ball was snapped on Theismann's final play. George's imitation was not bad. Not as good as Gil's, but not bad.

"Anyway," George said, continuing a conversation he had apparently initiated outside the car, "the Internet should belong to everyone. We've been too slow in bringing it to rural areas and the inner city. The very notion—"

"Why?" Andy said.

George wiped rainwater from his face. He lifted his eyebrows, perplexed, though not offended, by Andy's undemocratic spirit.

"Why?" Andy said. "It's just online shopping. It's just pornography. It's videos of two unlikely animals becoming friends. Why do the destitute require this? Who cares?"

Andy had meant to shut George up, but he realized his mistake immediately. There was nothing George relished more than the free exchange of ideas. What Andy had intended as a vicious, conversation-slaying remark was instead, he now understood by the look on George's face in the mirror, a generous and provocative strand in the complex braid of their constitutionally protected discourse. Andy could feel George's excitement emanating wetly from the backseat.

"I just read a fascinating study," George said, with the methodical force of a snowplow.

"George," Andy said.

"This lead researcher from the University of Illinois devised an ingenious study. What he did was—"

"George, are you married?"

"What?"

"Are you married?"

"Yes, by common law."

"Well, okay," Andy said. "I was married, see, and now I'm getting a divorce."

George made an extended sympathetic noise in the backseat. In the mirror Andy could see George wincing. "Andy, I'm really sorry to hear that."

"Yeah, well."

"Hey, man," George said, leaning forward and reaching his hands around the driver's seat. His left wrist got tangled momentarily in the seat belt, but eventually he was able to grip the tops of Andy's arms, and squeeze. Even if Andy had wanted to free himself from George's grip, he wasn't sure he could have. He could feel George's knees in the small of his back. He risked a glance, but George had the crown of his head resting on the back of Andy's seat, and he was no longer visible in the mirror. "Come here, man," George said.

"I'm here," Andy whispered.

"Tell me what happened."

This was a good configuration for Andy. This could work. As long as the windows remained fogged, as long as the rain made that sound on the thin roof of the car, as long as George's face was invisible in the mirror, as long as George gripped the tops of his arms and did not try to rub his shoulders, Andy felt that he could talk.

"One night last February—it was February twenty-third—we had dinner with some friends. There were two other couples there. We were having drinks before dinner. There was one of those uncomfortable lulls in the conversation, so I began to speak, just to end the silence. Another woman began speaking, too, at the same time, but then she laughed and said for me to please go ahead. I went ahead, George. I think about that now. I kept talking. I said that I had heard an interesting story on NPR. It was about these dinosaurs called oviraptors. The name means 'egg thief' or something."

"Yes," George said slowly. "Egg seizer."

"The scientist who discovered and named the oviraptor had found its bones on top of a nest of eggs. He surmised that the dinosaur was snatching these eggs, raiding the nest for food. But now scientists are taking another look at these creatures, and they think maybe this male oviraptor was not stealing the eggs, but maybe he was guarding them, being a good dad. Maybe he was taking care of the nest. And all this time, you know, he's been getting a bad rap.

"The other couples nodded and seemed interested. Not interested, maybe, but tolerant, and relieved at least that someone was speaking. Squeeze harder. But my wife was not happy at all. Julie. Her eyes kind of flashed, and she was just grinding cashews in her teeth, just grinding them to dust. She was drunk when we came. I was, too, I guess. She stands up, George. She stands up, puts her empty glass on the mantel, and says to the group that she had *also* heard an interesting story on NPR."

"Oh, no," George said softly into the fabric of Andy's seat.

"Yes, that's right. She said it was *fascinating*. It was a follow-up story, she said, about a recent ice storm in the Northeast. And they interviewed a tree expert who said that some of these big old trees—these majestic oaks and

elms and pines—these trees, the expert said, could sometimes have up to fifty thousand pounds of ice in them.
Fifty thousand. She kept repeating that number. Fifty
thousand. And she kind of pursed her lips the way she
does, and she tucked her hair behind her ear, and that was
it. We had dinner, we went home and had sex in the bathtub, and the next day she said she thought it would be best
if I would leave."

George groaned into the seat, and Andy could feel it in
his chest. George kept a tight grip on the tops of Andy's
arms. "That is rough, man," he said.

Andy nodded. With the windows fogged, he could not
see cars or men or hotel.

"But hey, listen, I think you probably know," George
said, "that the problems had been building up for a long,
long time before that night in February."

Andy stared at the dust on his dashboard. How does a
car get so dusty? "That is true," he said. He put his hand on
top of the Redskins helmet, which was sitting obediently
in the passenger seat. It seemed like a pet, an animate
thing, stolid and content and loyal. He wished he were
wearing it on his head.

"Andy, I've got some of my homemade stuff in a flask,"
George said. "You want some firewater?"

Andy said yes, realizing too late that George would
have to release his grip on Andy's upper arms to retrieve
his flask. Ungripped, Andy felt suddenly insubstantial,
incoherent. He took a big drink from the flask. Whatever
it was, was horrible, but he was grateful for it. When he

handed the flask to the backseat, he looked into the mirror and watched George drink. Andy noticed that George's thin gray hair, wet from the rain, was short and spiky on top. It was not pulled back.

"Hey," Andy said, "did you get your ponytail cut off?"

George nodded while drinking. Then he coughed into the back of his hand. "A couple of months ago, I saw a picture of myself on the library blog," he said. "It was taken from behind. And the next day I cut that thing off myself. It was time, man."

PETER TYPICALLY PARKED in the small lot at the side of the hotel. He had done it once as a mistake years ago, and now he maintained the practice out of his unarticulated sense that continuity was of a higher priority than convenience. A yellow sports car crouched dormant at one end of the nearly empty lot, far from the side entrance. The car was parked directly over a painted line, so as to take two full spots, proving once again to Peter that there are basically two types of people in the world. Though stationary and driverless, the car seemed contemptuous and reckless, with a wide, powerful backside. It seemed to *want* to break laws. It somehow gleamed without sunlight. In much the same way that he worried that his legs would fling his body from observation decks or scenic overlooks, Peter worried now that he would accelerate his Accord into the lean flank of the yellow sports car. He parked on the opposite side of the lot, pulling the emergency brake.

Since Peter used a side entrance, the men who had entered the lobby—even Robert in his stuffed chair—did not notice him. The woman at the front desk looked up and smiled at Peter as he passed, but he did not acknowledge her. He walked to the dining area, where he filled a cup with water at the juice dispenser. Upon opening the microwave he was momentarily stunned by the miasma of irradiated popcorn. He blinked his eyes against the vapors, steadied his legs. The interior of the microwave, like the interiors of all public microwaves, resembled the scene of a double homicide. He put the cup inside, closed the door, and programmed the oven to heat the water on high for one minute and fifty-six seconds. The start button was concave with history, like the stone steps of an ancient cathedral. The microwave rattled and popped. A dim interior bulb cast a faint yellow glow on the revolving cup and the spattered walls. A sign on top of the microwave, framed like the photograph of a family pet, asked that microwave users please demonstrate a respectful attitude toward fellow users. The clip art image on the sign, inexplicably, was of a guitar. Peter paced as the green digital numbers descended toward zero. He touched the new mouthguard in his pocket. On his phone he checked the weather, sent a text, renewed a prescription. He stood on his left leg, flexing his right knee. He had reached an age when a sore knee might mean either that the knee was sore, or that the knee was shot. He frequently had occasion to consider the phrase *bone on bone*. The microwave oven rattled along like some World's Fair exhibit. Could this really be, in our age, the fastest method for heating things up? Peter looked around, but there was nobody else in the dining area. A long banner above the continental buffet station welcomed Prestige Vista Solutions. On television, heavy wind pushed a car across a tennis court, eliciting nervous laughter and censored profanity from the amateur videographer. Peter ran his hand through his hair, which he had allowed to grow long in anticipation of a Saturday afternoon haircut from Carl. He did not particularly like Carl's haircuts, but he got one every year, and he worried that he would hurt Carl's feelings if he did not sign up. Peter stopped the microwave with two seconds remaining, and removed the hot cup of water. Then, following directions he knew very well, he dropped the new mouthguard into the slow boil. It floated there like a translucent semi-sessile annelid, the kind of tubular aquatic worm that is capable of regeneration. He left the guard in the water for slightly longer than directed, and instead of rinsing it quickly in cold water, as the instructions exhorted in bold font, he placed it directly into his mouth. He bit down hard, sucked vigorously to remove the air and water. He looked around, but there was nobody else in the dining area. The plastic was soft, and it tasted like synthetic butter. With his finger Peter pressed the scalding plastic into his gums; with his tongue he pushed the guard into the back of his top and bottom teeth. He sculpted the guard, made it his own. It was now unique. After a minute, which he counted more or less accurately in his head, he extracted the mouthguard and rinsed it in cold water from the juice dispenser. He put the mouthguard back into his mouth, and looked around. If the fit was not good, he could boil the mouthguard again. The fit was good, but he decided to boil the mouthguard again.

IN THE MEN'S RESTROOM off the lobby—frequently the subject of online reviews—the countertop and floor were wet, not as if an employee had recently cleaned them but as if firefighters had recently managed a blaze. A light above a corner stall was flickering dimly, reinforcing for Carl the correlation between luminance and civilization. In a brightly lit stall with the door closed, Carl pinched pills from his pocket and swallowed them without water. He reached beneath his damp Jim Burt jersey to touch the strange, tender bump that had recently appeared in his armpit, gently at first and then with painful pressure. The bump was hard, and it would not flatten or disperse with the force of his fingers. It seemed not to contain fluid. Perhaps he could show it to Charles, whom he knew to be a doctor of some kind. Hanging from a hook on the back of the door was the sort of brown canvas shoulder bag used by practitioners of the soft sciences. Carl removed the bag from the hook, and looked inside. He found two books, one called *A Better Mirror*, and the other titled *A Clinical*

Guide to Anorexia, 4th Edition. He dropped the books loudly on the wet floor, along with a thick three-ring binder, a day planner, and a manila envelope labeled "Protocols." In the front pocket of the leather bag Carl found a DVD with the handwritten title "Marla Sessions." He put the DVD into his coat pocket. He also took a large, pungent rubber band and a black Sharpie. He removed the top of the Sharpie and turned to face the broad blue partition of the stall. The surface was clean, though its gloss had been scuffed and dulled by solvents and abrasives. There was nothing on the wall to which to respond, no lewd conversational thread he could join with arrow and riposte. He didn't want to draw a dirty picture. He didn't want to insult someone's penis, or testicles. He didn't want to scribble song lyrics or to extol marijuana. The wall was so blank, so clean. He was committed to writing on it, but he didn't want to misquote Nietzsche or Camus. He didn't want to request a sexual act or to offer sexual services or to say anything at all about gays, blacks, Muslims, Jews, or God. He didn't want to post a threat. He didn't want to compose or transcribe a limerick about constipation. His shoulder began to ache from holding the pen aloft. The light above the corner stall flickered. The beginning was the most difficult part.

THE MEN CONGREGATED in the lobby, within the formidable purview of the enormous clock. Many held shoulder pads and helmets. Many had tied the laces of their cleats together, draped the laces over their shoulders. Gil demonstrated, with his hands, the size of the kitten he had found beneath his gazebo. Chad nodded, far more troubled by Gil's gazebo than by his kitten. Myron, with that startled look on his face, sought out Charles. Jeff tried to discern what seemed different about Trent, this year's commissioner. Trent had gained a lot of weight, perhaps thirty pounds, but the change was not remarkable. The men had reached an age when they gained and lost significant things in relatively short periods of time, and it was not unusual for someone to show up in November having acquired or divested weight, God, alcohol, sideburns, blog, pontoon boat, jewelry, stepchildren, potency, fertility, cyst, tattoo, medical devices that clipped to the belt and beeped, or huge radio-controlled model airplanes. The added weight seemed to coincide with Trent's leadership role, and it contributed to his authority as commissioner.

An aerial view of the lobby would have revealed more or less concentric arcs around the dry fountain, or perhaps around Derek, who was sitting, in flagrant contravention of a handwritten sign, on the fountain's edge. The general effect was not unlike the standard model of the atom. Randy, sitting glumly on a bench upholstered with a pattern of Eiffel Towers and poodles, was a distant outlier, as was the woman at the front desk, who was conducting Internet research on a bartending school called Highball Academy. ("We should totally do it," her friend had recently told her.) The men looked frequently at the clock, like pupils at a teacher. They looked occasionally at the woman, who so powerfully ignored them all. And they looked only rarely at Randy, who merely by sitting there unhappily collected from the beholder a kind of tax or levy in the form of an automatic withdrawal of sentiment. Randy was a figure who demanded the viewer's sympathy or disdain, and the other men resented having to make that choice, with all of its implications. To look at Randy was to have an aggressive confrontation with oneself, which was not what the men wanted this weekend, or ever. Randy's socks had lost their elasticity, of course, and they pooled lugubriously around black shoes whose heels had been wrecked by pronation. His herniated duffel bag lay at his feet. He had been unable to zip it completely, and in the unzipped bulge the men could have seen, had they been looking toward Randy, a small piece of the new and astonishingly white Jeff Bostic jersey. What most of the men had learned by now was that Randy's Bostic gear from the previous year had been stolen, according to Randy, from a self-storage unit outside of Wilmington, Delaware, and that Trent, using the discretion of the commissioner, had spent the dues money to replace the equipment rather than to rent out the conference room, which had been reserved by a baleful organization called Prestige Vista Solutions. What many of the men would suspect—and they would be correct—was that Randy, having lost his eyewear business, had sold the equipment in an online auction.

Jeff's check-in attempt had been rebuffed, and the other men thought it wise not to risk further attempts.

The woman at the front desk skimmed the FAQs at the Highball Academy site, and strands of her hair fell over her face like an *Out of Office* sign. She did not want to talk to the men about check-in. She disliked the notion that check-in time was flexible or negotiable, and she was strongly opposed to the men's duffel bags. She did not consider herself picky about men, but a duffel bag—she was sorry, that was just a deal-breaker. Her job, perhaps, had made her overly sensitive to luggage. She needed a man with a suitcase. No pleated pants, no exotic pets, no duffel bags—certainly there remained a sizable pool.

Wesley occupied the third arc with Bald Michael, Steven, and Nate. A very large canvas sack sat like a heeling dog beside Steven. The sack contained the lottery drum, enormous even when disassembled, that the men would use later that night to select players. Wesley had hoped to get a nap before the lottery. He had been having trouble sleeping for the past several months, and he typically felt exhausted in the afternoon. His entire life he had never had trouble sleeping, but all of a sudden he just couldn't do it. The insomnia made Wesley feel, biologically, like a failure. The family's pet cat slept twenty hours a day, and made it look easy. And now, granted many extra waking hours each night, Wesley had time to consider, for the first time, his other failures and shortcomings. Bald Michael was talking, Wesley realized, about his son, who just last week, Bald Michael said, began cruising.

"What?" Wesley said.

Bald Michael said that the kid already had a shiner and

a big scratch on his nose. "He's banging into everything," he said.

Wesley tried to conduct a quick audit of his discomfort. Steven and Nate did not seem troubled. Why did Steven and Nate not seem troubled? Why was Nate doing that strange crouched shuffling? One time, at a party, Wesley had overheard someone on a crowded patio explaining the customs of Fire Island, and it had made his toes curl. Then Steven did a pigeon-toed walk, and fell over. Why did Steven do that?

"No, like this," Bald Michael said, gripping the back of a chair and doing his own version of the walk of someone who was significantly injured or perhaps disabled. Nate and Steven laughed, so Wesley tried to laugh, too. Was Bald Michael making fun of the apparently serious erotic injuries sustained by his homosexual son?

"Hell, but what can I do?" Bald Michael said. "It's just a natural step. He has to go through it."

"And at least he's got a lot of padding," Steven said, slapping his backside.

Wesley studied them. He realized that if this was what it meant to be accepting, then he was not accepting. Bald Michael pulled a photograph from his wallet, and passed it to the men.

"Cute little guy," Nate said, passing the photo to Steven, who grunted his appreciation, and passed it to Wesley. The photo showed a toddler with a sweater vest and a chin rash. Wesley stared at the photo, and felt the sting of tears. He was so very tired.

"Wesley," Bald Michael said, "don't you have a boy, too?"

Wesley's boy was nineteen years old, and three inches taller than Wesley. He was a remarkable kid. He had not had a girlfriend since the eighth grade. Wesley felt that he and his son had not been close in many years.

"He's in college," Wesley said, though that fact sounded preposterous to him. "He's a pre-dentistry major, but he likes philosophy. He plays Ultimate Frisbee, which apparently is a serious sport. And he's probably gay. I think he probably is, though he hasn't said anything to me or to Barbara."

The third arc grew quiet. Bald Michael and Nate made sounds and faces that were intended to be supportive of Wesley's son's sexuality.

"It just seems like more and more people are," Nate offered. Bald Michael nodded. Steven's face did not look supportive at all, but in fact Steven had stopped listening. He had overheard a conversation about Redskins receiver Gary Clark in the fourth arc, on the far outskirts of the fountain.

"Excuse me, guys," Steven said, jumping like an electron to an outer shell. The men in the third arc assumed the worst about Steven. He was from Arkansas. Some people weren't quite ready for change.

"He wasn't a Smurf," Steven said to the men in the fourth arc—Trent, Peter, and Jeff.

"Who?" Jeff said.

"*Cahk,*" Peter said. "*Guhh Cahk.*"

"I clearly heard someone say that Gary Clark was a Smurf," Steven said. "And he wasn't."

"He had to be," Trent said. "He was tiny."

"*Fumbudge den*," Peter said.

"He was small, but he wasn't one of the Smurfs," Steven said. "The Smurfs were Virgil Seay, Alvin Garrett, and Charlie Brown. And that was before Clark was drafted out of James Madison."

"*Cahk uz pot uv fumbudge*," Peter said.

"Take out your mouthguard," Jeff said.

Peter removed his mouthguard, which remained umbilically connected to his mouth by a thin strand of saliva. "Clark was part of the Fun Bunch," he said.

"Wrong again," Steven said with gleeful exasperation. "The Fun Bunch dissolved after the '84 season. The league made the rule about excessive celebration, and that all but wiped out the Fun Bunch. Excessive celebration, you may recall, was pretty much the Fun Bunch's reason for being."

"I think the key term here is *orchestrated*," Trent said.

"Ready?" Jeff said. He bent his knees and swung his arms, counting to three. It appeared that he wanted to reenact the Fun Bunch's group high-five, but the other men ignored him, and Jeff did not leave the carpet.

"Wait," said Gil, who had leaped two levels to join the conversation. "Did the Smurfs and the Fun Bunch exist at the same time?"

"The Smurfs were basically a subset of the Fun Bunch," Steven said, drawing circles in the air. "Contained within the superset of the Fun Bunch was the Smurfs, who were the Fun Bunch's smallest receivers. Think of it like this: all Smurfs belonged to the Bunch, but not every member of the Bunch was a Smurf."

"Was that thunder?" Jeff said, looking toward the parking lot.

"Gary Clark was part of the *Posse*," said Myron, materializing out of some unknown arc with a startled look on his face.

"Correct," Steven said. "*But not in '85.* Clark, Art Monk, and Ricky Sanders were the members of the Posse, but Sanders wasn't a Redskin until '86. There was no Posse in '85. It didn't exist. Guys, I explain this every year."

"So what group did Clark belong to in '85?" Trent said.

Jeff stared at the woman at the front desk.

"Nothing," Steven said. "No group. That's what you have to keep in mind."

IN THE MEN'S RESTROOM off the lobby there were six urinals across from three stalls. Vince entered the restroom, regarded the six unoccupied urinals, and selected, for reasons ultimately too complex to comprehend, the second urinal from the left. He placed his free hand high above his head, palm against the tile, in the manner of one being frisked for weapons. Though alone, he suppressed a sigh. Fat Michael then entered the restroom, and he chose a urinal, the fifth, at a suitable but not gratuitous distance from Vince's. He made this calculation instantaneously, without conscious thought, while whistling "The Coventry Carol." This spatial arrangement was conventional and propitious, provided a third man did not enter. Gary entered, and he discerned the dreaded 2-5 split, by which means two men in essence had occupied an entire wall of urinals. With reluctance he chose the third urinal, to the right of Vince, and immediately began talking.

"My wife would like me to piss sitting down," he said.

Fat Michael nodded, staring at a piece of blue gum in his urinal that resembled a brain. His wife, too, had asked him to sit down. It was not an unreasonable request. The validity of the request, in fact, was what had made Fat Michael so angrily opposed. Danish men sit down, she had told him, which only made him more recalcitrant.

"She doesn't like the mess I make," Gary said. "She says men in other countries sit down."

"Do they?" Fat Michael said.

"I don't know," Gary said.

On several occasions through the years, when afternoon sun was illuminating the bathroom in a soft and golden light, Vince had seen his urine splattering out of the toilet while he stood. Honestly, it was like a fireworks show. There was no denying it. His wife, too, had asked him to sit. She had read something about Sweden. When he finished at the urinal, Vince turned and saw, on the glistening floor of the middle stall, a brown canvas bag and two books.

"I tried sitting once," Gary said. "I did. I was trying to

be considerate. Because one time, when the sun was slant-
ing into the bathroom at the perfect angle, I could see the
piss just shooting out of the bowl. Have you ever seen those
salmon when they return to their spawning grounds?"

Of course, of course the other men had seen the
salmon.

"It does make a mess," Gary said. "But the one time I
tried sitting, the only time, my dog came into the bathroom. He's this old, handsome black Lab with a grizzled
snout. You know what I mean?"

Fat Michael and Vince nodded, solemnly affirming
the way that old handsome Labs become grizzled in their
snouts.

"He just looked at me," Gary said. "And I honestly think
he was judging me. I was down at his level, sitting on the
toilet, and I just think he totally lost respect for me. I could
see it."

"I don't think your dog was judging you," Fat Michael
said. He turned from the urinal, eliciting the ferocious
automatic flush. On his way to the sink he noticed,
beneath the door of the stall, the brown canvas bag and
the books.

"I just couldn't do it anymore," Gary said.

"You really should," Vince said, though he did not.

"What do you think, Charles?" Fat Michael said at the
sink, scrubbing his hands like a surgeon.

"Hey, Charles," Vince said, knocking on the door of the
stall.

"Doesn't he work with young girls?" Gary said.

"Settle this one, Charles," Fat Michael said. "Was Gary's dog judging him?"

"Charles, do Danish men sit?" Vince said. He knocked again, harder, pushing the door open and revealing an empty stall and a comprehensively vandalized partition. Vince entered the stall, followed by Gary and Fat Michael.

"Holy crap," Gary said, facing the wall.

"Wow," Vince said.

This happened a long time ago. In high school i used to go out drinking with my friends and then late at night i would sneak over to this girl's house to have sex. She wasn't even my girlfriend. I would throw gravel at her window to wake her up then she would come downstairs to let me in. She would close the door and then lie down on the rug in the foyer. She was so tired. Why would she let me in? Do not write slut. Imagine being woken up for sex by a drunk boy who doesn't love you. ~~*What i'm trying to*~~ *one night i was throwing rocks at the window and then another window opened in the back of the house and her father stuck his face out and said oh for god's sake just come in! I went back home instead. The night was ruined. Do not write faggot. I told myself i would never go back there again but i went back several more times. Do not write hell yes. Do not draw a vulva. Someone should have put me in a kennel. All of us. Her name was stacy demps and i'm sorry. Do not write pussy.*

Gary laughed, patting his front pockets, his back pockets.

IN THE LOBBY, the model of the atom had collapsed into a tight cluster of men that moved gradually, and without the volition of its constituents, toward the front desk. Tommy's mustache made Robert uncomfortable—it was a statement in a language that he did not understand—and so Robert broke from the cluster, and retreated to the locked door of the conference room. There was, he recalled, the year that Chad tried to break-dance atop the long, gleaming table. Once again Robert checked the foam board schedule on the easel beside the door. The room was still booked for the entire weekend. The repaired chinstrap dangled from his long flannel cuff like a chrysalis. He did not like change, which he experienced nearly always as loss. He felt forlorn about the conference room, and exasperated at Randy, and bitterly envious of Prestige Vista Solutions.

Jerry, the director of transportation for Prestige Vista Solutions, checked the schedule on the easel beside the door, but he saw only a scribbled sketch of a fish. He asked

Robert if Robert was one of the football players that he had seen in the lobby. Yes, Robert said quietly. He did not want to talk, or to explain, particularly to this man with a laminated name tag. The name the Redskins had given the flea flicker play was the Throwback Special, and thus some of the men, never Robert, referred to the group as "specialists." Neither did Robert care for the term *reenactor*, which made him think of the freaks with hardtack and muskets, running through the woods and endeavoring to keep their powder dry. There was not a good way to talk about what he was doing here.

"It's an annual thing," Robert offered. Jerry stood beside him, facing the locked conference room. From the lobby behind them came the waves of masculine sound, the toneless song of regret and exclamation. Then, like a child handling an item he has been forbidden to touch, Robert said, "But this is the last year." He rubbed the inside of the chinstrap with his thumb, stared at the honeycomb carpet in the conference room. "Last year," he repeated, rubbing the strap. There, he had said it, though he did not know why. He had no idea if his claim was true. Its truthfulness was somehow beside the point, as he had not intended to disclose or predict. He had intended something else, some reckless spell or counterspell, he did not know. Robert suddenly felt dangerous to himself, and he glanced at Jerry to gauge the potency of his remark. It was something of a relief and a disappointment to observe that Jerry seemed undisturbed.

Jerry had seen the jerseys and helmets in the lobby,

but had no idea what the men were here to do. He asked Robert if Robert remembered when Lawrence Taylor broke Joe Theismann's leg on *Monday Night Football*. Robert said yes, he remembered. Compound fracture, Jerry said, wincing. A comminuted fracture, as well, Robert said. His voice was too high, and honestly, why was he talking at all? A comminuted fracture is when the bone breaks into several pieces, Robert explained. The men stood side by side, staring through the small window of the door of the conference room. Now Robert worried that Jerry was going to tell a story about the night it happened. Strangers who saw the helmets and uniforms always wanted to tell a story about how a friend's mom fainted and the bowl of popcorn just went everywhere and you could see up her skirt. Or about the friend, now serving time, who laughed when Theismann's leg broke in two. Or about how they were doing geometry homework, and the sound was down so they didn't hear Frank Gifford say, "Theismann's in a lot of trouble," and they didn't hear Gifford say, "We'll look at it with the reverse angle, one more time, and I suggest, if your stomach is weak, you just don't watch," and they didn't hear *Monday Night Football* color commentator O. J. Simpson groaning at the violence, and they happened to look up and see the reverse angle, and they either threw up or they very nearly threw up. Jerry told Robert he would always remember Lawrence Taylor's reaction. Yes, of course, Robert said, hoping to curtail Jerry's memories. After having snapped Theismann's fibula and tibia, Taylor frantically waved for the medical personnel on the Redskins sideline to come onto the field. And then he stood with his hands on his helmet. Did Robert remember? Robert did. And there was something about that gesture, that very human gesture, an archetypal sign of despair or disbelief, holding one's own head. For comfort, or perhaps for protection or containment. Except that Taylor still had his helmet on, Jerry said, staring through the small window of the door of the conference room. He would never forget it, Jerry said. So his hands, Taylor's hands, rested not on his forehead or scalp, but on his helmet. The circuit of anguish could not be completed. The very equipment of his profession was an impediment to his humanity, to the proper expression of shock. Jerry from Prestige Vista Solutions did not say *circuit of his anguish*, but it's precisely what he meant. Robert understood. He nodded. He did not want Jerry to have the conference room this weekend, and he didn't particularly want to be standing here talking to Jerry about Theismann, but nevertheless, everything Jerry had said was correct.

TRENT HAD COME HOME to find his daughter going down on a boy. Jeff had come home to find his daughter going down on a girl. Andy had come home to find his kid doing like this with an aerosol can of whipped cream.

"Yeah, whippets," said George, the public librarian.

Tommy had come home to find that his dog had eaten a package of diapers. The surgery was twenty-five hundred dollars, and now he had pet insurance. Nate had come home to find his wife Skyping with a man in a military uniform. Bald Michael had come home to find his son hurting a cat. Whenever Peter comes home now, his daughter is reading. He was so anxious for her to learn to read, so worried when she showed little interest, but now that's all she does. She doesn't even talk to Peter anymore. She just sits in corners, knobby knees pulled up to her chin, the book held over her face like this, like a veil. The other men knew about books over the faces of girls. Carl came home to find his son building something with a lot of wires. Wesley came home to find that his twins had built twin snowmen. The picture was on his phone if he could only find it. Fat Michael had a friend who came home to find that the rags he had used to apply linseed oil to his furniture had spontaneously combusted, causing sixty thousand dollars of property damage. When Steven had come home, everyone in the house was just gone.

"My mother is living with us now," Gil said. "One day I came home and I didn't see her anywhere. I checked the backyard, but she wasn't there. I came back in, looked in the guest room, in the den, in the basement. She wasn't there. I was calling out for her, but there was no answer. Then upstairs I find her in the bathroom. We have those sliding glass shower doors. You know what I'm talking about?"

"They slide like this?" Steven asked.

"No, like this," Gil said, though Steven looked skeptical. "And the doors had broken. They had just shattered. Later I looked online. Apparently, this happens. They sometimes just explode into thousands of pieces of glass. On their own. It was nothing my mother did."

"I've heard of that," Andy said.

"The glass was inches thick in the shower and all through the bathroom. It seriously looked like a beach in there. My mother was in the shower when the glass broke, and she couldn't move. She couldn't go anywhere. She would have sliced her feet up. So she just stood there wrapped in her towel, trapped in the shower for I don't know how many hours. She wouldn't really say."

Charles, who typically did not care for Gil's unseemly stories about his mother, began to look around the lobby for his brown canvas bag.

"Her voice was hoarse," Gil said, "presumably from calling out to nobody. She looked like she was shivering, but she said it was just her palsy. You know what she said? She said it really wasn't that bad because it gave her some time to think. That's what she said. Time to think. I tried to clear a path through the glass. I swept the shards into a dustpan. I filled a garbage bag with *glass*. I cut my hands and knees. I was bleeding and sweating into the glittering pieces of glass. I said, 'Mom, goddamn it, just say it was a bad day!' I said, 'Mom, this is bad! Just say it!'"

The woman at the front desk held a wince against the drone and pulse, the loud achievement of assembly. Soon the men would disperse, leaving behind in the lobby their scent and those curvilinear bits of dried mud that had fallen from their silly football shoes. She said it looked like the rooms were now ready. "Five total, is that correct?"

"Six," Andy said.

"Oh, yes, six," she said, squinting at her computer screen. "And have you gentlemen stayed with us before?" she asked.

Andy stared at the mole on the woman's cheek. He knew there was another one on her abdomen, just below her right breast. He felt incorporeal.

"Yes," he said. "Every year for the past sixteen years."

- 2 -

THE LOTTERY

"**'H**AIR ON A MAMMOTH IS NOT PROGRESSIVE IN any cosmic sense,'" George said to Rick, a copyright lawyer for Prestige Vista Solutions.

"Okay," Rick said, looking at his shoes.

"That's Stephen Jay Gould."

"Is it?" Rick said.

"What he means," George said, stepping into the elevator with Rick, "is that there is no inherent or *objective value*—good or bad—to the woolly mammoth's thick hair. The hair becomes valuable, or not, only within a specific context or environment. Only in an ice age would hair be favorable. Only in warmer temperatures would it be deleterious. The woolly mammoth is not, cosmically, a fit creature, and neither is its hairless counterpart. Fitness, always, means fitness within particular environmental conditions. It's not as if you could look at both and predict which one would survive."

Rick pushed his floor button, then pushed the door close button several times. He shifted his weight back and forth from left foot to right.

"Gould provides an interesting analogy," George said slowly. "So you said, what, that the flea flicker was a *horrible* call. Well, yes and no. I would argue that you need to consider a play in its context, its environment. And the environment of a play is, to a large extent, the opposing team's play. A play can take its form—and value and fitness—only within the medium, the crucible, of the adversary's play. What we call a play in football is actually the reaction that occurs between two plays, which up to the point of the snap are just competing abstractions, just fantasies of domination. To call a play is simply to transmit information."

George was pacing the car. Rick stared at the illuminated and unchanging numbers above the doors. The elevator stopped, and its doors opened to an empty hallway. Rick resolved to write an online review of these elevators.

"The plays that are called from the sidelines are speculative, abstract. The line of scrimmage is the narrow barrier between those abstractions. When the ball is snapped, the barrier dissolves and the two plays begin to act upon each other. We have confluence! From two plays the play comes into being. Each team's playbook fantasy takes on terrestrial form. The play lives a fleeting life, like certain unstable isotopes. Each play attempts to assert dominance over the other play, by force and deception. This is why football is the most scientific of sports. A game is a series of discrete experiments. Hypothesis, observation, results, analysis, conclusion."

The number 5 button was illuminated, but Rick jabbed

it eight or nine times. Rick's simple point in the lobby, which he now regretted making, was that if your quarterback's bone comes out of his leg during a play, then it was a bad play.

"The Throwback Special was not *a priori* a bad play. Or what did you say? Dumbshit? A *dumbshit* play. You can't say it was a dumbshit play merely because it didn't work. That's a tautology! The trick play happened to be catastrophically bad on that unseasonably warm evening on natural grass on a first and ten from near midfield against the Giants' charging linebackers, who were drawn in, it is true, by the handoff to Riggins. And of course one of those charging linebackers was Lawrence Taylor, who was really a kind of player the league had never seen before. Taylor himself could make a lot of teams' plays seem, what you said, *fucking asinine*. But every play is in fact a limitless number of plays, depending on contingency. Not just the opponent's play, but injury, wind and weather, field conditions, crowd noise, execution, personnel, and all of the special properties of the compound that is created by the two constituent plays. Bye. Peace. This was fun."

REALLY, any container of appropriate size would have worked just fine. An ice bucket, a duffel bag, an empty case of beer. Just something large enough to hold twenty-two ping-pong balls. In the early years, the men used whatever was handy, and there were never any problems. But eight or nine years ago Steven showed up with a huge lottery drum that he had built in his basement. The spinning drum rested on a detachable metal frame constructed of heavy metal poles that screwed together. The drum itself was a Plexiglas barrel with a small latched door on one end, and a superfluously large crank on the opposite end. The barrel would have held four hundred ping-pong balls. The commissioner spun the drum with the crank, then unlatched the door, reached into the barrel (often up to his shoulder), and drew out a ball on which was written one of the men's names. One half of the drum was painted blue and red, with a Giants logo, and the other half was painted burgundy and gold, with an impeccably rendered Redskins logo. Consequently, the drum was ugly. The paint seemed to be coated with a scratch-proof, high-gloss polyurethane. The two halves of the drum, like the poles of the frame, could be taken apart for storage and transportation, though the disassembled unit remained gigantic and unwieldy. When assembled, the lottery drum was immense and foreboding, just far too massive and ornate and shiny for its simple purpose. Steven kept the dismantled drum and frame in a canvas sack, and the kit was commonly mistaken, even in a hotel, for a large camping tent. The men joked that the canvas sack would work just as well as the drum it contained. The men, almost all of them, strongly disliked and disapproved of Steven's lottery drum. They could not, it is true, fault the design or the construction. Well, yes, they could. That was exactly what they could fault. The drum was too fancy. In fact, several of the men called it Fancy Drum. It was, after all, simply a tool. "It would be like, what if I decorated my jigsaw?" Wesley said one year, though in fact he did not own a jigsaw, or any other power tools, and always had his boards cut by the grumpy associates at Home Depot after waiting twenty humiliating minutes in the wood-cutting area, during which time the automated female voice on the store intercom said, over and over, "Special assistance needed in the wood-cutting area." The men, most of them, despised Fancy Drum based on their sense of propriety or rectitude or congruity or harmony or aptness or accordance or seemliness or fitness or meetness or concord. The drum's crank, it was evident, had been polished. "God, there it is," one would whisper to another. "I hate that thing." Countless threats against Fancy Drum had been made in the past several years, and consequently there was no real surprise, and no clear suspect, when one of the poles for the frame went missing.

"That pole was here two hours ago," Steven said to Trent, sitting on the floor of Room 324, searching the canvas sack once again.

Trent asked if the drum had been in Steven's possession the entire time. He asked if the item was insured. He asked if Steven felt he could definitively rule out those human resource reps from Prestige Vista Solutions.

"It's not funny," Steven said.

"You know," Trent said, "the drum was always great in the conference room where we had plenty of space. But this year, in here . . ."

The lottery was being held this year in Room 324. The room had two queen beds with diamond stitch comforters, an orange sitting chair, a desk, a dresser, a television, a mirror, a bedside table between the beds, a standing lamp, and four sconce lights. Above one bed was a framed watercolor of fireworks over a lake. Above the other bed was, as far as Andy could tell, precisely the same framed watercolor of fireworks over a lake. He stood between the beds, staring first at one painting, then the other, looking for minuscule differences. There were no differences that he could see.

Beneath the window was a heating and cooling unit that ticked and clanked. Trent had parted the window curtains, both the heavy, scratchy primary curtain and the gauzy, membranous under-curtain so popular in hotels. The windows overlooked the dark wet parking lot. It was still raining.

Most of the men had not yet arrived in the room for the lottery. They were resting or showering or watching television in their temporary rooms. Here in 324, Gil lay on one of the beds with his eyes closed. He needed a haircut. Trent flipped through a three-ring binder of laminated menus. Steven found the missing pole for the drum's frame.

"Here it is," he said.

"The remote control," Myron said, "is the dirtiest item in a hotel room."

"Dirtier than the sheets?" Chad asked.

Andy turned from the watercolors, and there commenced a discussion of the meaning of the idiom *Fish or cut bait*, which all of the men were accustomed to hearing. Trent thought it was basically synonymous with *When the going gets tough* or maybe *If you can't stand the heat*. Myron was under the impression that the expression meant that one should just do something, anything. Get involved. If you don't want to fish, fine, but then you should at least help those who do want to fish by preparing their bait. Trent wanted to know exactly what kind of bait required cutting. Steven, sitting on the floor and assembling the frame of the lottery drum, said everyone was wrong. Trent assured the men that the keg was on its way.

The heating and cooling unit ticked and clanked. Gil's leg twitched. That guy. His father had been a French horn player. He could sleep through anything. The men—Trent, Steven, Andy, Chad, and Myron—felt compelled by tradition to go ahead and try the shaving cream trick on Gil.

"THERE YOU ARE, Charles," Nate called from the foot of the crowded bed.

Charles was sitting on the bed, leaning against the headboard. He waved negligibly to Nate. The room was hot and loud. The men around the bed compared their devastating commute times with a kind of pride, converting liability, momentarily, into triumph.

"Could we step outside for a minute?" Nate said.

"No," Charles said.

Nate slid between Randy and Wesley, and then shuffled down the narrow alley between the wall and the bed. "I'm glad you're here, Charles."

"I like those boots," Charles said, wondering what size they were, and whether Nate might give them to him in barter.

Nate looked down at his boots and shrugged. "Robert said I was not responsible for my thoughts," he said. "But that doesn't seem right to me."

Charles could not comfortably make eye contact with Nate from his seated position. His neck ached when he looked up at such a severe angle. He felt like a child, or a baby bird. This was no position from which to adjudicate pathology. Nate had a hairy throat, and a strong, though not unpleasant scent. Charles was the expert here, and this would not do.

"Switch places with me, Nate."

Nate climbed over Charles's legs as Charles spun them toward the wall, and stood. "Excuse me, Gil," Nate said. "Sorry about that."

Now Nate sat against the headboard, and Charles stood beside and above him. This was much better.

"You can help me, right?" Nate said.

"Yes," Charles said, "I can."

"What I said to my wife was that I was curious. That's all I said. Sexually curious about them. And she acted like I had a *big* problem."

"Slow down," Charles said.

"Sexual curiosity is completely normal, right?"

"Generally speaking, yes," Charles said.

"That's what I told her," Nate said. "That's exactly what I said."

"But it does depend to some extent," Charles said, "on the object of your curiosity."

"What?"

"About whom are you sexually curious, Nate?"

Nate looked across the crowded room. He waved, though Charles could not see anyone waving back. Then Nate turned his face toward Charles's hip. "The women in children's books," he said quietly.

"I didn't hear you, Nate," Charles said, though he had.

"The women in the children's books I was reading to our kids."

"I see."

"The illustrated women. You've seen them, right?"

"Some."

"I mean, they're *women*. There they are with breasts, hips, legs. The illustrators made them, not sexy, I guess, but definitely feminine. And I suppose technically speaking, these are not all human women I'm talking about. Some are squirrels or mice or rabbits, but they are female and they walk upright and they're gentle, and in the drawings we see their housecoats and blouses and the definite suggestion of the female form. I wouldn't say this about just any creature in the woods on a nature show. I'm not interested in animals."

"What are you interested in?"

"These characters in the books have had children, so you know they're sexually active. That's not some sick thing I'm imposing on the book. And in some of these old books the mothers are so . . . Like in *Blueberries for Sal*? Do you know that one, Charles?"

Charles said that he did know *Blueberries for Sal*.

"So lock me up," Nate said. "That mother is definitely someone I'm curious about."

"The woman," Charles said, "or the bear?"

"The way McCloskey crosshatched her long skirt? That's all I'm saying, Charles."

"And her sweater," Charles said.

"I guess one thing I'm saying is that in trying to make these drawings not at all risqué or suggestive, the illustrators made them very risqué and suggestive. Does that make sense?"

"Go on."

"I read the books to our kids, and occasionally I am curious about the women. Or the female animals. I didn't say attracted to them. I didn't say turned on. I said curious. The drawings are not indecent, and I would say my thoughts are not all that indecent, either. We have this old book that belonged to my wife when she was a kid. It's my favorite. It's about an elephant."

"In terms of my expertise—"

"There's this scene in the book when the elephant is performing at a circus, and there is a crowd of delighted people in the bleachers behind the ring. And if you look really closely, Charles, you can see these women sitting in the bleachers. They're wearing tight knee-length skirts, and they have nice figures, and they look happy. Almost ecstatic, Charles. The picture isn't vulgar, but . . . it stimulates the imagination. I've read the book a thousand times. I notice the women behind the elephant, right? Big deal. I think about their sexual histories. I wonder what they like to do in bed, either alone or with others."

"And this is a drawing?"

"Colored ink. The old four-plate process, I think. But fairly realistic. It's clear how happy the women are."

"Okay."

"And yes, these women are depicted at an elephant show, but we know that's not all there is to them. We know they have a private life that is off the page, away from the circus. So that makes me a pervert? Their sexuality seems to me to be, I don't know, part of them. Right? It's not something I . . . It seems . . ."

"Intrinsic?" Charles said.

"No," Nate said.

"Yes," Charles said.

"It's not like it's something I would ever act on," Nate said.

Charles pressed the back of his head against the wall. He had no idea what that would entail. "Why did you tell your wife?"

"I just pointed out the women at the elephant show," Nate said. "I don't know why I did that. She didn't seem to understand."

"I've seen this before," Charles said, and Nate looked up at him with an expression that shifted from surprise to relief to disappointment. The room was hot and agitated. "You are processing this experience as sexual, but it is not."

"Yes, it is," Nate said.

"It's not sexual," Charles said, trying to earn the boots. "What you find provocative is the women's happiness, and their privacy. You're longing to know them, and they are concealed. Your curiosity is not fundamentally erotic. There's nothing wrong with you, except the normal stuff."

"But I look at their breasts," Nate said.

"Your mind," Charles said, "strives to put these images and feelings in a familiar context."

Nate suddenly seemed despondent. He would rather, it occurred to Charles, have been diagnosed as an untreatable pervert than as someone who was just lonesome. Apparently, he had forgotten that he had sought out Charles for reassurance or explanation. Nate had finished talking, and it also appeared that he had finished listening. He seemed miserable.

Charles rested his hand on top of Nate's head. He watched as Gary, Vince, and Fat Michael tried to carry the lottery drum across the room. Fat Michael just happened to be wearing short sleeves (in November), and the cephalic vein in his bicep bulged tyrannically. Go to sleep, all you pussies, Fat Michael's cephalic vein said to the men who had gathered in Room 324. Sweet dreams.

"Where?" Gary shouted to Trent. "Bathtub or hallway?"

Then the keg came through the door. It advanced into the entryway, but stopped when it saw the lottery drum directly in its path. The lottery drum halted but did not give way. The keg and the lottery drum squared off in the narrow strait of the entryway, beneath the looming form of the ironing board. Myron looked startled, but he always did. The quiet standoff lasted perhaps a minute. This was not to be decided by feints or clever maneuvers. The men cheered as the keg lurched forward.

THE RULES AND RESTRICTIONS of the lottery, formulated by Steven at its inception, were simple, clean, and egalitarian: Each man writes his initials on a ball, and places the ball into the approved container. When all balls are mixed in the container, the commissioner draws each of the twenty-two balls, one ball at a time. The man whose ball has been selected then has three minutes to choose any available player from either team. The following restrictions apply: (1) you may not select a player who has already been selected; (2) you may not select the same player twice in any five-year period; (3) you may select a player from the same team for no more than three consecutive years; (4) you must serve on the Redskins offensive line (which includes tight end Donnie Warren, but does *not* include tight end Clint Didier) at least once every five years; (5) you must serve in the Giants defensive backfield at least once every seven years; (6) you may not select a player whose physical dimensions are so radically different from yours as to inhibit your performance or to introduce basic issues of credibility (this restriction is enforced by the commissioner); (7) you may not choose Lawrence Taylor more than once in any eight-year period; (8) you must make your selection in a timely way, or it will be made for you by the commissioner; (9) you may not select a "toucher" (Donnalley, Riggins) in consecutive years, or the year after being Theismann; (10) you may not, of course, select Theismann. The man whose initials are on the final ball remaining in the container will be Theismann. None of the rules for selection (above) apply to the player who is selected as Theismann.

The lottery drum had been damaged in its encounter with the keg, and it lay on its side in the hallway outside 324. An IT associate and two graphic designers from Prestige Vista Solutions examined the drum warily, as beachgoers inspect a washed-up animal. The IT associate, Josh, asked the other two if they remembered when Lawrence Taylor snapped Theismann's leg in the Super Bowl. The graphic designers nodded, though they were too young to remember. Their grisly cultural touchstones were much more recent, and high-def. "I had mono," Josh said. The two young men nodded. "Well, wait, so I guess it couldn't have been the Super Bowl. Plus the Giants and Redskins can't play in the Super Bowl. Never mind. Maybe I was thinking of Tim Krumrie. Remember when Tim Krumrie's leg snapped, and kind of flapped around in the air in the Super Bowl?" The two young men nodded.

The keg was stationed just inside the room's door, on top of several thin gray hotel towels. Some of the men by the keg were reminded of the skirt of a Christmas tree, and this association, far from merry, was for them unhappy. The men by the keg were also outside of the bathroom, and they heard an almost constant cycle of urination, flush, and wash. Carl, filling his cup with beer, said it sounded like a car wash in there.

"Guys?" Trent said.

"Okay, guys?" Trent said.

The room was hot, and very crowded. The pizzas and breadsticks had been delivered, and exchanged for a moist wad of bills that due to an accounting error had included a sixty-eight-dollar tip. The room now smelled of sweet tomato sauce and warm meat. The pizza guy in his rain-slick red windbreaker had asked, upon entering, if this was a bachelor party, and Gary had said that it was, and Steven had said that it wasn't, and Peter had said something incomprehensible through his mouthguard.

"Lot of men in here," the pizza guy had said, pocketing the large wad of bills and planting himself on the corner of a bed.

Randy, who had sold his Jeff Bostic equipment at Internet auction and then lied about it, was in the corner, as alone as it was possible to be in a hot room packed with men. Derek stood in another corner, ardently surrounded. Bald Michael was standing on one bed, using two breadsticks to dramatize a boating accident he had witnessed last summer. All of the men, almost all of the men, licked the sauce from their fingers.

"Should we begin?" Trent said.

"Guys?" Trent said.

"Hey," Trent said, waving a ping-pong ball above his head. "Guys."

"Guys, should we begin?" Trent said.

"Let's go ahead and get started," Trent said.

"Guys," he said.

Someone did one of those whistles that requires either two fingers from one hand, or one finger each from two hands. Probably Carl, who had once coached soccer.

". . . pyramid scheme!" Vince shouted into the silence that ensued after the whistle. The toilet flushed. Bald Michael's breadstick, being driven by a drunk teen without a boating license, stalled in the water high above the queen bed.

"Anyway," Gil murmured, "it's a farmhouse sink. The thing is one hundred and fifty pounds."

"Anyway," Tommy said quietly, "the walls are plaster, so there are those strips of wood lathe underneath."

"Anyway," Robert whispered, "after that, I shelled out for snow tires."

"Long story short," the pizza guy, smoothing the bedspread, said to Andy, Chad, George, and Jeff, "I met my wife about ten years ago through an online dating site called Firestarters. We hit it off, we got married a couple of years later, we had two kids. Things were going fine. I had a good job as a consultant for a company that installs geothermal systems. Everything was fine."

George, who was eager to know more about geothermal systems, gave enthusiastic nonverbal listening cues to the pizza guy.

"People sometimes ask me if it was a good marriage," the pizza guy said. "And I'm like, compared to what? It was fine. We lived in the same house. We grilled on the patio. We selected paint colors. We bought stuff from the neighborhood kids who came to the door. Fine. So then last January we get a letter in the mail. It's a check for one hundred and seventy dollars, made out to both of us, along with a letter explaining that the check is a payout from a class action suit that we didn't even know we were a part of. Turns out that the guy who ran Firestarters had gone to jail for fraud. He hadn't actually matched people together based on their profiles, using what they'd called sophisticated algorithms of affection. There were no algorithms. There wasn't even a computer. In the Firestarters office? You know what they found? Twenty cases of diet soda and a color printer and a big bulletin board full of headshots. This guy and his staff just matched people together based on their pictures, without any consideration of other information about pet allergies or ideal vacations or religious affiliation, et cetera. And even though his success rate was as good as any of the other top dating sites, he went to jail, and there was a class action suit, and all of the defrauded couples got a check."

"That's a sweet deal," Jeff said.

"When I first found out, I was excited. It was a jolt. Like, okay, you and me, honey, we're outside of science here. We're off the grid. This isn't about being a city mouse or a night owl or a neat freak. It was like a new start. It was like we could start over, almost like we were strangers. The thought that we had not been united by a computer I found exciting, and even kind of sexy. It was exhilarating to think that we may or may not be well suited for each other in terms of temperament or retirement goals. It's like I suddenly had a mistress, but the mistress was my wife. It really spun my head around. No algorithm! But listen, guys, my wife had completely the opposite reaction. She said she suddenly felt that she did not know me at all, and she said that made her frightened. Wow, I didn't think anyone actually used that garlic dipping sauce. She said she was scared of me, this big stranger in her home. My big boots, my big parka. And she said that this news just validated certain suspicions that she had had over the years about how truly incompatible we are."

Trent was saying something. Andy, George, Chad, and Jeff leaned perceptibly toward the pizza guy. None of the men would have necessarily considered the pizza guy *big*.

"She said she had never truly been happy, but she always thought the problem must be with her. She said the science, the computer, had intimidated her. She said she knew it sounded silly, but she believed if she had left me she would have been leaving reason and common sense. And so while I'm excited by all this, she starts flinching around me, and pressing her back against the wall every time I walk by. She starts sleeping in the guest room, and when I go there to smell her clothes and sheets, I find a kitchen knife under the bed. She was acting crazy, which was attractive to me because one of the things that had always bothered me about her was how completely measured and reasonable she always was. So now she was unreasonable, and I loved it, but when I moved toward her, she got even more scared and unreasonable, which I found almost irresistible. And we fought all the time, which was exciting, but it became clear that she in some way considered me—and not the convicted founder of Firestarters—the fraudulent and deceitful party. The whole marriage just disintegrated in a really exciting way immediately after that crappy little check arrived. In April—early April—she asked me to move out. So I moved out."

"That is some story," Andy said. He patted the pizza guy on the shoulder, and made his way toward the keg. Chad chewed on the inside of his lip, considering whether or not to tell the story about the nest of mice in his dishwasher.

"Late June, she calls me one day, out of the blue, completely frantic about a noise in our chimney. Her chimney. It's loud and it's low down, directly above the damper. She said it was a loud chittering sound, and she thought it was a squirrel or a raccoon or a bat. She held the phone to the fireplace, but I couldn't really hear anything. She said she was sorry to bother me, but she didn't have anyone else to call. So I went over there to the house we used to live in together. I didn't mind. I was happy to see her. She had a weird new haircut, but she looked nice. After a few minutes by the fireplace, I heard the noise, a very agitated chirping sound. Really loud. My first thought was squirrel. My wife sat on the love seat behind me with her laptop."

"Guys?" Trent said.

"She was trying to find audio recordings of different animals stuck in chimneys. She played them. She apologized again for calling me. I said it wasn't a problem. I put on my big work gloves, and maybe she had that scared look again. She said, Hold on, does it sound like this? She played another recording of an animal stuck in a chimney. All the recordings of stuck animals sounded like the animal stuck in our chimney. Every one. I got a cardboard box from the basement and I put it inside the fireplace. She said to hold on, she wanted to look up a few more things. I squatted down, and I used the poker to open the damper. When the damper opened, I threw down the poker and got ready to close the flaps on the cardboard box when the squirrel fell out. Wait, my wife said. Don't do that. At first nothing happened, but then all of a sudden—plop plop plop—three baby birds fell into the box, squawking and cheeping. And then I could hear the mother bird up in the chimney, making all kinds of noise. Now of course the mother bird sounded exactly like the recording of birds that my wife had played on her computer. It's birds, I said. My wife said, I told you to wait. She read to me from her computer. She said they were chimney swifts. She said they're common in our area. She said they would have flown the nest in another two to three weeks, all of them, mother and young. There had been no need to do anything. I could have left them alone and they would have been fine, but now what? We both looked down into the box. The baby birds were wet-looking, and covered in black dust. Their eyes weren't even open. Christ, Henry, she said, they're federally protected! I took the birds outside in the box, I don't know why, and then a while later I brought them back in, so at least they could be close to their mother. My wife paced around the room, and then she got back on the love seat with her laptop. She was leaning way over, her hair nearly touching the screen. She said, Please don't do anything. Just don't do anything at all. She found something online. Plenty of other people have had baby birds fall out of their chimneys into a box. The thing to do, she said, is place them gently back where they came from. They will try to clutch you with their claws, but they will not hurt you. Try, she said, to reach above the damper and place them on the wall of the chimney. They like to be on a vertical surface. I thought you weren't supposed to touch baby birds, I said. She said, Just put them back! They're *federally protected*. I took off my gloves and one by one I picked up the baby birds and placed them back into the chimney, above the damper. They did grip my fingers with their claws, which made it difficult to let them go. But I did it, and then I closed the damper. The mother and the babies made a terrible racket for a while, but then they all got quiet. Everything seemed to be okay. My wife closed her laptop. She stood up from the love seat, and thanked me for coming, though she wouldn't look at me. My hands were black from the soot in the chimney." The pizza guy looked down at his hands. "I told her I thought we made a good team. We saved those birds, I said. She said, We saved those birds from the danger that you created for those birds. Which, she said, feels pretty familiar. Then I left."

"What happened with your consulting job?" Chad said.

"Long story short," the pizza guy said, "the next weekend I was down in the basement. I would come in through the bulkhead, sit in the old rocking chair that used to be in the nursery, and just listen to my wife and kids upstairs. I liked to hear them. This night they were playing Yahtzee—my son, my daughter, my wife, and some man named Kent I had heard a few times before. It's *my* Yahtzee game, by the way. I've had it since I was a kid. They were playing in the living room, and every time they shook the dice in that cup, the birds in the chimney went nuts. They clearly were thriving. They chirped like crazy at the dice, and then my family and Kent all laughed and laughed like it was the funniest thing. I could hear my daughter say, They like it! And then Kent said, Or they don't! Laugh, laugh, laugh. Now who's the fraud? Now who? And that's why I went upstairs, and that's how this whole thing got started."

"Guys?" Trent said.

"Chad? George?" Trent said.

"Jeff?" Trent said.

"Take it easy," the pizza guy said, and he left. He had another delivery.

"Guys, let's do this," Trent said.

•

FANCY DRUM lay capsized in the hallway, but really, any container would have worked just fine. With mock altruism several men simultaneously offered up the use of their capacious jockstraps, while Gary suggested Vince's purse.

"It's not a purse," Vince said.

Someone stripped a pillowcase off a pillow, and the case was passed hand to hand up to Trent, who stood in front of the television. Trent began to transfer ping-pong balls from a large freezer bag into the pillowcase. Some of the balls were yellowed like teeth. Four or five of the men tried quickly to formulate a joke about Trent's weight, and Gary got there first. "Don't eat them, Trent!" Gary yelled, just as Bald Michael was about to do his Cookie Monster voice. Trent smiled mirthlessly, patting his stomach. The weight had simply come with his third marriage. His habits had not changed. He hadn't stopped going to the gym, hadn't altered his eating or drinking. This was just who he was in this marriage. With his first wife he had been an outdoorsman; with his second wife he had been really into live music, and he had smoked a pack of cigarettes a day; with his third wife, apparently, he would be overweight. From what Trent could gather online, his first wife still enjoyed the outdoors, as did her current husband.

When Trent had finished dropping the ping-pong balls into the pillowcase, he gripped the opening as one would grip the neck of a large bird, and he gave a trial shake. The soft clacking of the balls in the case was pleasing, and several men closed their eyes to hear it better. It is true, however, that many men felt the absence of the lottery drum, though they knew it to be ridiculous and excessive. The drum, like the conference room, had become part of the way things were done, and its excess, it might be said, had become part of its necessity. It was, perhaps, after all, appropriate. Not just any container would have worked just fine. More than one man had the odd sensation that a lottery without the drum somehow wouldn't *count*. Others felt exposed somehow, or denuded by the loss of ceremony. This anxiety caused them to be garrulously nonchalant about ceremony.

"RIP, Fancy Drum!" Myron called out, raising his red cup of beer. "Let it never be said she shirked a fight."

"To Fancy Drum!" the men said, and drank. Several men slapped Steven on the back. This small tribute was composed of a complex alloy of sincerity and derision, the ratio of which was a dark mystery to every man present. Still, it was sufficient for Steven, who stopped pouting, and accepted the attention with a smile and a raised cup. It could be said of Steven, as it could be said of each man, that he was the plant manager of a sophisticated psychological refinery, capable of converting vast quantities of crude ridicule into tiny, glittering nuggets of sentiment. And vice versa, as necessary.

"She'll be back," Steven said.

"Yes, she'll be back . . ." Gil said, raising his arms like a choral conductor.

"But she won't be back tonight!" the men shouted on cue.

"Let's keep it down," Robert said.

Indeed, the men were boisterous. Peter chewed his mouthguard, feeling the strain, poignantly familiar from a childhood spent salvaging curbside furniture, of making do.

Traditionally, the commissioner said a few words before starting the lottery. Nothing formal, nothing prepared, just a welcome, maybe a joke. The men grew quiet. Trent slung the pillowcase of ping-pong balls over his shoulder. This posture, combined with Trent's recent weight gain, and perhaps with the thin hotel towels beneath the keg, and possibly also with the experience of waiting anxiously for a special annual event that would be over all too quickly, necessitating a return to normal life, evoked for some men the image of Santa Claus. Trent shifted his weight from foot to foot. His face glistened with sweat and tomato sauce, and he unconsciously wiped his forehead with the pillowcase. He removed from his back pocket a wrinkled piece of paper, then used his mouth to unfold the paper. This was one of the worst things that could have happened, and a wave of agitation passed through the crowded room.

"I've written an invocation," Trent said. "A rhyming invocation." He cleared his throat. "Now, if you would, please bow your heads."

The men, all of them, stared into their cups. They could hear the tap of the cold rain on the window. This was quite possibly going to be worse than the year George was commissioner, when he circled the conference table, speaking slowly about the freedom of assembly, the value of ritual, and the theory of play espoused by Dutch cultural historian Johan Huizinga. He had touched all of the men as he passed their chairs.

"What a devout group of assholes," Trent said, laughing. He balled up the sheet of paper and threw it at Myron. "Come on, let's do this. Carl?"

Carl, still wearing the Jim Burt jersey, turned off the sconce lights above the beds, and turned on the projector, which he had made from a shoe box, a magnifying glass, and his phone. In this way the men could see, projected onto the wall above the television, the "board," or list of players available for selection, which Carl would update after each man's turn. Although this jury-rigged projection system was resourceful, and not vastly inferior to the system in the conference room, it nevertheless caused some mild embarrassment.

"Bravo, Carl," Tommy said.

"Focus!" Andy said.

Trent lowered his hand into the pillowcase, first grazing the ping-pong balls gently with his fingertips, then plunging his fingers into the mass, scooping and mixing, rolling them across his moist palm. He pinched a ball (Chad's) between his thumb and forefinger, then dropped it. He selected another ball, and gingerly lifted it from the sack like an egg of the endangered loggerhead turtle. Before looking at the name on the ball, he held it aloft, presenting it to the room.

"God, I think that might be mine," Bald Michael whispered from the open door of the bathroom.

It was as one would expect: Some men in the room fervently wished to have the first selection. Gary was one of them. George. Wesley, strangely enough. Carl. Steven. These men wanted a full board, a large menu. They knew what they liked, and they were not frightened of options. And then there were other men who desperately did not want to choose first, who were at this moment, this and every year, filled with a sense of dread that their initials were on the ball in the commissioner's hand. The prayer that they silently prayed was the same one they chanted as children beneath beds or behind woodpiles: *Please, let me not be found.* From the hallway came the sound of ice spilling violently into a bucket. Randy was one of these men. And Tommy. Robert, for whom choice was oppressive. Myron, like all Myrons. Bald Michael, who became paralyzed in the well-stocked aisles of supermarkets or home improvement stores. And perhaps especially for Derek, whose anxiety about the lottery, this and every year, was unique and complicated. Derek was concerned—nearly to the point of nausea, in fact—about the thorny psychoracial thicket into which he, a mixed-race man, would be plunged if the commissioner called his name. He could, with the first pick, *just choose Lawrence Taylor.* Throughout the years, most men had chosen Taylor with the first pick, either because they genuinely wanted to be Taylor, the prime mover of the drama, or, in one or two cases, because they worried what the other men would think if they did not choose Taylor. (In those years the reenactment had been marred by a mincing and tentative antihero.) But

Derek had always been vaguely troubled by the portrayal of Taylor as villain—or, more accurately, as monster, a kind of soulless, inexorable beast who laid waste to Caucasian linemen on his way to the wavy-haired former Notre Dame quarterback who was dating Cathy Lee Crosby. Who leaped almost supernaturally onto Theismann's back—who *jumped* him, basically—surprising Theismann at home at night in the safety of his pocket. Not content merely to sack Theismann, but intent on destroying him, snapping his bones, ending his career. Taylor as black devil, as bogeyman. A noble savage, at best. For the men, Derek thought, Taylor offered the opportunity not only to sublimate their roiling, middle-class aggression, but also to take a transgressive racial thrill ride. Not an emphatic immersion but a ritualized, sanctioned projection of fear and disgust. In a helmet, in a jersey, their volatile subconscious had an outlet that seemed both safe and dangerous. Was Derek making this all up? Of course Taylor had truly been a ferocious and relentless player who scared the daylights out of offensive players and coaches, but Derek could not help but feel a twinge of distaste about the way that some of the men played Taylor, with a kind of wild-eyed, watch-your-daughters primitivism, licensed both by Taylor's revolutionary abilities and, unfortunately, by his considerable off-the-field troubles. Granted, you could not portray Taylor with the workaday, gap-toothed brutality of the archetypical white linebacker (Butkus, Nitschke, Lambert, Ham, Urlacher), but one needn't venture into minstrelsy, either. So Derek, were he to choose first, could choose to choose Taylor, seizing the role for himself, rejecting caricature and adding nuance. He could modify, adapt, and deepen the portrayal, providing a model for those who followed. He could play Taylor with ferocity, but also with dignity and humanity and intelligence, and in this way he could perhaps subtly instruct his peers. But seriously, even if he could somehow see his way toward some authentic vision of Taylor, both distinctive and emblematic, did he really believe that he, a lone man with a righteous cause, could enact change? What kind of fantasy was that? Derek noticed for the first time that George had cut off his ponytail. And if he were thinking in terms of exemplum or emblem, wasn't he already far, far away from an authentic and idiosyncratic representation of Taylor? Unless of course being a symbol was integral to Taylor's particularity. Unless, that is, Taylor himself was playing a role, and so to portray Taylor was to take on the role of a role, to act like an actor. That sounded right. That sounded like being black. Wasn't it true that Derek, too, felt at all times like both a distinctive person and a representative, man and mannequin? What would more likely happen, Derek knew, was that the role would seize him, and not the other way around. By choosing Taylor, he would create—reveal? create? reveal?—a metadramatic racial tension. Though light-skinned, Derek was black, and here he would be, irreducibly, a black man choosing Lawrence Taylor.

The ball there in Trent's hand, held above his head. The quiet of the room. That chintzy projector, projecting far more than the board. Well, and of course the angry black man would select the frightening black man. And now look, the entire group of men would be made uncomfortably aware of the racial dynamics of reenactment, which was good because white people needed to be far more aware of the subtext of race. Which was terrible, because they were all here to have fun. Derek, too. This was one of his favorite events of the year, even if the other men tended to come on a bit strong. He liked being part of the group, studying film, wearing the uniform. He liked the collective pursuit, each man doing his job so that that play could be successfully catastrophic. So why was he doing this? What was his problem? Why did he insist on turning something fun into a grave American ordeal? What kind of pathology seeks to diminish pleasure and play? Oh, and Derek just *knew* how it would look if he chose Taylor. Here he had been, playing along for years, lying in wait, biding his time patiently, yearning for his opportunity to play Taylor, to (re)enact, symbolically, racial vengeance not just upon Theismann and the Redskins—good Lord, they were named the Redskins—but upon the man playing Theismann, and upon the whole group of men, and really upon all white people everywhere. It was so obvious that Derek would choose Taylor, for at heart he was just an angry black man. Which he wasn't, because he would not be reduced like that. Which he was, because who wouldn't be? Selecting Taylor—it was so clear—would not be an opportunity for racial healing and gentle instruction, but an outright act of hostility and aggression. He,

Derek, would not control the meaning and significance of Lawrence Taylor's sack. Centuries of American history would control the meaning and significance of Taylor's sack. It was the worst kind of soft, sentimental thinking to imagine that an individual by force of will and conviction might provide . . . Plus, Jesus, he detested the thought that such a vexed decision would be regarded as such an obvious decision. And never mind the profound rhetorical challenge of actually uttering his selection of Taylor, of speaking it to the group in a hotel room. If he said it forthrightly, confidently, he would create discomfort and fear. If he shucked and jived to comfort his peers, he would activate his dormant self-hatred. And there were other variations—should he pause, appear to be uncertain— each of them fundamentally dishonest. So okay, over the years it had become pretty clear to Derek that he could not choose Lawrence Taylor, lest he convert the Throwback Special forevermore into a charged racial allegory (which it really already was!), and convert himself from one of the guys to type and ambassador (which he really already was!). But Derek knew that not choosing Taylor was also a decision laden with significance. If he selected another player, he would not be primarily choosing that player; he would first and foremost be *not choosing Taylor*. He would in essence be renouncing Taylor and all that Taylor represents. It would be an evasion, a denial. A betrayal? The not-choice would resound as a choice, and quite possibly as deficiency or fear. And whom would he choose instead? He had worked it out many times. He could be black Giants safety Kenny Hill. Yes, he could station himself as far as possible from ball and bones, could in fact move away from the collapsing pocket, far beyond the camera's eye. He could excise himself from the historical record. That would be a forceful racial statement indeed. Or he could be black Giants linebacker Harry Carson. He could charge with Taylor, swell the progress. He could get to Theismann first, make him step up in the pocket, prepare him for comminution. But that would look to all like Derek wanted to be involved, but could not handle the heavy symbolic burden of Taylor. Or hell, he could go white! This was his way out of the conundrum. This was the escape hatch. He could be Didier! He could be the Redskins second tight end, a beefy Caucasian named *Clint*. That would show them all! It was devastatingly clever. It was Derek as trickster, subverting the group and the performance through ironic appropriation. Or something. But Derek was not convinced that choosing Clint Didier or any of the other *seven* white Redskins would actually expose or undermine the system in any meaningful way. It would probably just look odd, and perhaps even cowardly. It might look like he was trying to pass. It might arouse pity. It might appear to be another instance of racial self-loathing. Or it might after all actually *be* another instance of racial self-loathing. With the first pick—there was no way around this—you were either Lawrence Taylor or you were not Lawrence Taylor, and both choices were fraught. There was no other option. Derek wanted to take a large drink from his beer, but he worried his hand would shake. He was relatively certain that none of the other men, not even Charles, had ever considered the racial dimensions of the lottery, and he knew they would not unless and until the year that Derek's name was called first. No, not even then. It would not be until Derek spoke, until he chose, at which point Derek would be guilty of introducing an ugly topic into a fun and friendly tradition. He was desperate for the ball in Trent's raised hand to be his ball, and also for the ball not to be his ball.

Trent lowered the ball to his eyes. "Gary," he said.

The men applauded and whistled. Several men nudged Charles in the arms and ribs, presumably because chance had now given way to psychology, Charles's métier.

Derek regarded the intricate patterns of the carpet.

"Hmmm," Gary said, rubbing his chin and gritting his teeth and staring up at the ceiling in a grotesque pantomime of indecision. The men laughed and told Gary to fuck off.

"L.T.!" Gary shouted, beating his chest with his fists.

OUT OF HABIT, Robert checked his watch, but failed to perceive the time. He looked up, squinting into the shabby light of Carl's projector. How is one to live? When Robert helped his wife prepare a nice meal, he invariably thought of all the dishes they would have to wash later. When he loaded the car for his family's summer vacation to the beach, he thought of how unpleasant it would be to unpack the car a week later. Even if the family vacation was "fun"—and often it did contain pleasurable moments for Robert—it would soon be over. *While it was happening it was ending.* As soon as the vacation began, it was eroding. How do you enjoy something that has, by virtue of beginning, commenced its ending? How, for instance, do you put up a Christmas tree? (All those fragile ornaments, wrapped in tissue.) There was in fact no beginning, or middle. It was all end. How silly, then, to load the car, to drive eleven hours for something that was just going to be gone. Wouldn't it be easier to remain at home? That's where they would end up a week later, with their sunburns and sandy towels and a thousand digital pictures of that time—which year was that?—that they went to the beach. Everything that had happened to Robert in his life was over, and the things that had not yet happened were on their way to being over. Some would be over sooner, others later. He often looked forward to watching a game on television, but when the game started, it was ending, and so he could not enjoy the game. Robert glanced at Charles, who was scratching his armpit. He wondered whether Charles was respected by peers. When Robert heard a song he liked, he was aware that the song was dissolving in time, second by second. I like this third verse, he would think. Here comes the third verse. Here it comes. Then the third verse just evaporated. What did it even mean to like a song? There was no song. The song wasn't there. It was just like that cocktail in the screened-in porch after a day of hot sun at the beach, the happy pink children eating watermelon, the handsome and serious wife reading a frivolous magazine, her feet propped up, her toenail polish flaking, a breeze coming through. It wasn't there, either. Anything good that would happen to Robert would be converted instantaneously to something good that had happened. And something good that had happened was, because it was already over, something somber.

Tommy, who seemed to have withdrawn behind his mustache, was on the clock for the second pick of the lottery. The men waited, while Tommy rubbed his temple and squinted at the unfocused list of players projected on the wallpaper. There were, it should be said, different "schools of thought" regarding a post-Taylor selection. This was what the men said. They conceived of "schools of thought," so that their decisions would be attributed not to their own deeply rooted and wholly individual fears and psychoses, but to an established external system. These schools of thought only very slightly resembled the real categories. Some men, for instance, just did not want to be on the offensive team. To be a Redskin, even a blameless wide receiver, was, for these men, to don the tainted uniform, to participate willingly in a campaign of spectacular demise. They would rather be the most insignificant player on a pillaging defense (e.g., Terry Kinard) than a Redskins player who was essential to the calamity. Other men, those who had taken drama in high school, or those who danced willingly at weddings and office parties, found a kind of tragic nobility in ruinous failure, and they

were inclined to spend high lottery picks on Redskins players in the pocket, close to ground zero, even or especially
those players who do their jobs poorly. Members of another
group, who willingly allowed themselves to be mistaken for
members of the previous group, were drawn to Redskins
players out of a keen, if unrecognized, identification with
disappointment and culpability and bumbling malfunction.
Some other men were simply averse to periphery. These
men did not care what uniform they wore. They wanted a
central role, and they tended to select the most prominent
and involved player remaining on the board, Redskin or
Giant. There was of course a shadow group, whose members craved the familiar comfort of anonymity and insignificance—and feared responsibility and centrality—and
yet tended to overcompensate for this shameful desire by
choosing the most significant player available, and thus
appeared to crave centrality and import. A couple of men,
those with large contributions to their 401(k) plans, almost
every year made an unexciting pick in preparation for next
year's selection. A final group, which consisted only of Steven, was composed of the dilettantes and aesthetes, men
who chose players based on very specific and idiosyncratic
qualities of uniform (tape, towel, wristband, face mask,
cleats) or stance or movement. For these men, the play was
not the thing; the play was not essentially communal, nor
was it tragic or allegorical or even violent. The significance
of the play was that it provided an opportunity to approach
perfection by matching one's own appearance and move-

ment to a historical model. The small white towel tucked into Perry Williams's pants, his crouch as he lines up across from Art Monk wide left, the strange jiggling dance he performs while waiting for the ball to be snapped . . .

The bland optimism, high ceiling, and corporate sterility of the conference room would probably have mitigated the effects of Tommy's facial hair, but here in the hot and crowded hotel room, his mustache acted as a pernicious depressant. A few men's thoughts returned unpleasantly to the complicated and contentious eleventh-hour custodial negotiations that had allowed them to come this weekend. Without looking directly at Tommy, the men waited for him to make the second pick.

"Take your time, Tommy," Trent said not unkindly, looking at the curtains. Trent's comment had the effect not of putting Tommy at ease, but of making him more anxious. The toilet flushed, and the inordinately brief span between the flush and Gary's emergence from the bathroom suggested that he had not washed his hands.

Tommy, overcompensating for a shameful desire to be insignificant, chose Redskins running back John Riggins, whom Jeff had once called "the vice president of the disaster."

"Riggo!" Gil shouted.

"The veep!" Nate shouted.

"The Diesel!" Chad shouted.

"Well, yes and no," Steven said. "The Diesel at age thirty-six, in his final year in the league. His yardage was way down."

Riggins, along with center Rick Donnalley and Theismann, was a toucher. The Throwback Special was a flea flicker: Theismann handed to Riggins, who then pitched back to Theismann, who was then supposed to throw a forward pass but instead was broken into pieces by Taylor. Tommy, who this evening had already spilled two beers and a piece of pizza, had not considered that he would be handling the ball.

Trent picked Gil's ping-pong ball from the pillowcase, and Gil, who had not been on the Redskins line in the past four years, was compelled by rule to select a lineman. Scowling, Gil chose right tackle Mark May, whom he considered not a good selection but the least terrible selection, given his options. Bald Michael, who had been Mark May three times, and Andy, who had been Mark May last year, made eye contact across the room. Gil was disappointed now, but he wouldn't be for long. Once you had played May, you understood.

With the fourth pick, Nate chose Giants linebacker and South Carolina native Harry Carson, whose chinstrap Robert had mended carefully and now did not want to relinquish. Then Bald Michael and George, perhaps in an attempt to bask in reflected glory or perhaps because they wanted to share a room with Gary and Nate in the Fracture Compound, chose the other two Giants linebackers, Gary Reasons and Byron Hunt, respectively.

"Borrowed plumage," Robert muttered to Derek, whom he generally tried to avoid out of respect.

Derek, uncertain how to respond, raised his empty cup to his mouth.

There was some rowdy chatter about the Big Blue Wrecking Crew, as well as the Crunch Bunch. Steven, acting quickly, was able to douse the enthusiasm with historical fact.

Randy, sitting glumly in the orange chair, selected Redskins tight end Donnie Warren with the seventh pick. He just said it, with no hesitation. Donnie Warren. His mind, apparently, had been made up. The men grew quiet. They could not recall Warren ever being selected in the top ten. Steven would have to check his notes. Warren's job on the play is to help protect Theismann's tibia and fibula from blindside pass-rushers. Though an eligible receiver, he remains at the line to help left tackle Russ Grimm handle Lawrence Taylor. But Taylor, as it turns out, deposits Warren on the grass in a biodegradable heap on his way to Theismann. Warren is the breach point. And his one-on-one battle with Taylor is not, it must be said, particularly noble or stirring. He is not elevated in defeat. It is difficult to locate the grandeur. Last year Randy had been left guard Jeff Bostic, and now here he was, voluntarily sliding two spots toward mayhem's gate. Randy had, in the winter, lost his eyewear business, and he had sold the Bostic gear at Internet auction. Then he had claimed, in a largely incoherent, inconsistent, and self-pitying late-night email to Trent, that the gear was stolen from a storage unit near his home in Dover, Delaware, at which point Trent had reluctantly purchased new Bostic gear with the dues money. But now Randy seemed to be accepting culpability, albeit ceremonially, by choosing one of the players most culpable for Theismann's monstrous injury. This was the only explanation for Randy's pick. You didn't have to be Charles to get it. Traditionally, the men made oinking and snorting noises when a Redskins down lineman was chosen, but the men were too surprised to snort, and the room remained quiet. From the hallway came the sound of ice spilling violently into a bucket.

"Heavy is the head," Andy whispered, even though it made no sense.

"The pick don't lie," Vince whispered, more to the point.

AS THE LOTTERY PROGRESSED, as his ball remained in the pillowcase, Derek began to consider the possibility that Trent would select his ball last. That would make things interesting indeed. What if Derek were Theismann? How would a black Theismann— But no, Trent pulled Derek's ball from the case, giving Derek the sixteenth motherfucking pick. The men applauded. Why? Why were they clapping for Derek and his shitty pick? Were they relieved that he would not be Theismann? All that was left for Derek, of course, was a choice between some fleet-footed Negro in the Giants secondary and some grunting Redskins trench dweller who almost certainly enjoyed bow hunting in the off-season. Derek squinted drunkenly at the blurry board. There was Perry, Terry, Kenny. Or there was Rick, Clint, Ken.

There was a knock on the door. A number of men flinched and grimaced at the sound, and several even seemed to duck or crouch furtively, as if in an attempt to conceal themselves in a small room containing more than twenty men. A couple of men reflexively put their index fingers to their lips. A couple of men pressed themselves flat against a wall, and seemed to hold their breath. Myron found himself gripping the window curtain. A knock was bad.

In loud falsetto Gary said, "*Who is it?*"

"Guys, it's me," a voice said.

"*Hold on,*" Gary said. "*I have to locate my panties.*"

"Open up, Gary," the voice said.

Gary looked through the peephole. "It's just Adam," he said. "I didn't see him leave." Gary opened the door, and Adam entered the room.

"Jesus, it's hot in here," he said. "Why aren't we in the conference room? I went there first, and there was some other group in there."

The men stared at Adam, realizing for the first time that Adam had been missing all day. Now that they saw him here, it was obvious that he had not been here. Adam. Good old Adam. He looked good. Not very good, really, but the same. Not bad. Just like Adam, like himself.

Medium build, dark bags beneath his eyes. It was nice to see that guy. Not nice, but normal, customary. Though, honestly, it was disconcerting for the men to realize that they had not previously noticed Adam's absence, as it suggested to each man the possibility that his own absence might go unnoticed here. Far more seriously, they suffered a kind of retroactive anxiety about the missing man. He was here now, but he hadn't been here. He very well might not have come, a fact they had not considered before but were forced to consider now, even though he was here. His arrival should have comforted them, but in fact made them more apprehensive. Several men began counting men.

The men gave Adam a hearty greeting. They said they knew he'd make it. Where had he been?

"Don't ask," Adam said, taking off his wet jacket and pumping the keg with vigor.

"We waited as long as we could," Trent said.

"Seriously," Gary said, "where were you?"

"I mean it," Adam said. "Do not ask."

"Get yourself a beer, Adam," Gil said, though Adam already held a full cup in his trembling hand.

"What did I miss?" Adam said. "Why are we in here? Why is Fancy Drum in the hallway? Who's L.T.?"

After the knock on the door, someone had bumped Carl's projector, and the phone had toppled inside the shoe box. Derek, though, had memorized his options: Perry, Terry, Kenny. Rick, Clint, Ken. He knew, when he thought about it, that he wanted to be in the Redskins huddle. In his experience that huddle was a grave and sacred gathering. Something happened in there, and he wanted to be a part of it. While nobody seemed to be listening, Derek chose Clint Didier. He announced it quietly, to nobody, and Steven recorded it.

"Almost Indian summer weather here in mid-November," Vince said in a terrible Frank Gifford impersonation.

"You sound Chinese," Jeff said.

"Gil, you do it," Vince said. "Gil's is great."

"Why is Carl wearing Burt?" Adam said. "Is there any pizza left, or did Trent eat it all? Why didn't you wait for me?"

Someone tapped Derek on the leg. He looked down to see Randy, sitting glumly in the orange chair. Randy tapped him again, and Derek leaned over.

"You'll wear the black gloves," he said confidentially.

"What?"

"Didier wears the black gloves," Randy said, holding up the backs of his hands.

It was not clear to Derek whether or to what extent this despondent liar with the tragic socks was aware of Derek's intense ambivalence about the racial implications of the lottery. Did Randy get it? Was he trying to fold Derek gently back into the community? This glum bankrupt with the patchy beard—he was either offering something to Derek, something humane and real, or he was just fetishizing sports gear.

"And the elbow pad on your right arm," Randy said.

Derek nodded, involuntarily cupping his elbow with the palm of his hand.

"WHAT DID I MISS?" Adam said. "Who's still on the board? How does that projector even work? Is this really what we're doing this year?"

Myron chose center Rick Donnalley, and the men snorted and oinked. Adam chose Giants cornerback Perry Williams. Charles selected Giants safety Terry Kinard, who lines up deep downfield and cannot really even be identified in extant video of the play. Peter chose what sounded like Giants safety Kenny Hill.

"I'll see all three of you in Vegas," said Chad, who earlier with the thirteenth pick had selected Giants left cornerback Mark Haynes. "Vegas" was the name given to the hotel room shared by the defensive backs, presumably because their distance from the sack, their relative unimportance in the play, constituted a license for debauchery and mischief.

There were just two balls remaining in the pillowcase, Trent's and Fat Michael's, and one player remaining on the board, Redskins right guard Ken Huff, traditionally a very late selection because he fails to block linebacker Harry Carson, who then chases Theismann into the pulverizing embrace of Taylor. The men at this late juncture considered the possibilities. The next man selected would be forced to take Huff, and the final man would be Theismann. Trent would have made a decent Theismann as recently as last year, but now his weight was an issue in terms not only of verisimilitude, of course, but also of agility. The man who plays Theismann must be nimble and adroit; he must step up into the pocket to avoid the man playing Harry Carson, then he must crumple convincingly when mounted by the man playing Taylor. You had to be fairly athletic and dexterous to suffer a simulated compound comminuted fracture, and everyone knew that Trent would have been a terrible Theismann. There had been unconvincing Theismanns in the past—Tommy always came to mind, as well as George—but perhaps none who had seemed so clearly unfit to play the role. The rain tapped the windows.

Trent bit his lip, dropped his glistening forearm into the pillowcase. The room was quiet as he drew out a ball, then read his own name. His ensuing gestures and expressions of disappointment were pretty obviously feigned. Similarly relieved, the men all looked at Fat Michael. His body was so excellent that he could tuck in his shirt, and he had. He looked like one of the figures cavorting athletically on ancient Greek earthenware. What would it mean to break Fat Michael, to cut him down, albeit ceremonially? Some of the men realized that they had wished for the wrong thing, that Trent might have been the preferable option.

Fat Michael appeared to blanch, though it could have been the sconce light that Carl turned on after shutting down the projector. Theismann's iconic helmet was produced from a duffel bag in the corner, and it was passed hand over hand across the room to Fat Michael. Following custom, Fat Michael put the helmet on, and the men cheered and whistled, slapping his shoulders and the top of his head. With just its single crossbar, the face mask did not mask Fat Michael's face. Everyone could see it. He made his way around one queen-size bed and over the second. The men parted, making room for him to pass. He went into the bathroom, closed the door, and turned on the fan.

"And guys," Trent said.

"Hey, guys," Trent said.

"And guys, remember," Trent said, "if history offers us any lesson at all, it is this: do *not* hang your jerseys on the sprinklers!"

The men bellowed merrily at Andy, who, a decade earlier, had been the protagonist of the year the sprinkler went off. The misadventure had been a kind of gift to the community, and Andy was subsequently regarded as a major donor. Those who were close enough to punch him in the arm punched him in the arm.

Out in the hallway Fancy Drum was gone.

- 3 -
NIGHT

THE DEFENSIVE BACKFIELD WAS IN ROOM 212 (Vegas). The defensive line was in 256. The touchers were in Room 324. The offensive line was in 432 (the Sty). The receivers and tight ends were in 440. The linebackers were in 560 (the Fracture Compound).

Gear exchange was a chaotic and inefficient and lengthy and primitive process. Over the years there had been several sensible, even elegant, proposals for a more orderly exchange, but each had been ignored. As they did every year after the lottery, the men now roamed hallways with helmets, shoulder pads, and uniforms, searching for the men who required their gear, as well as for the roaming men who had the gear that they required. The cumbersome burden of the equipment was essential to the rite, as was the notion of quest, as was the act of bestowal, as was the inebriated sociability among fellow wanderers. "I hate to say it about my own kid," Nate told Vince in the stairwell, "but he's about the sickliest little thing I've ever seen." In the fifth-floor hallway, Robert, having received downstairs the pristine Jeff Bostic gear from Randy, bestowed his Harry Carson gear upon Nate. "Carson," Nate said, wiping his palms on his pants. Robert could hardly expect Nate to notice the mended chinstrap. In fact, if Nate noticed the chinstrap, it would probably mean Robert had not repaired it well. And he had repaired it well. When Robert was a child, his father had told him that there is never a need to draw attention to one's own accomplishments. People notice a job done well, his father had said, but in Robert's experience that had not been true. What people notice is tardiness, failure, moth damage. Robert's father had been a corporate whistleblower who was pilloried in the press. He now lived alone in rural Illinois, where he sat erectly in a folding chair, listening to police scanners. He carted around an oxygen tank, but still had the power to humiliate Robert.

Nate pinched the Carson jersey at the shoulders, and extended it in front of him. Then with both hands he held the jersey to his nose, and inhaled. He nodded, tossed the jersey over his shoulder. Robert handed Nate the shoulder pads, which Nate clacked twice with his knuckles, and placed on the floor. Next, Robert extended the pants, the interior pockets of which Nate examined for knee, thigh, and hip pads. Finally, Robert handed Nate the helmet, upside down, the chinstrap curled inside like an hors d'oeuvre in a bowl. The long hallways seemed somehow not to be uniformly lit. There were, along the corridor, small patches of darkness. Around a corner came the grave murmurs of bestowal, the clacking of pads. The vending alcove clicked and hummed. The elevator rumbled. Nate peered down into the helmet. He gripped the chinstrap, rubbing its soft interior with his thumb.

Startled, Robert began to back away. "What you've got to keep in mind, Nate," Robert said, imitating Steven, walking backward rapidly toward the elevator, feeling, for reasons he did not fully understand, *shame*, "is that Harry Carson is from South Carolina."

JEFF SAT on the floor of the vending alcove, talking on the phone to his son.

"Is this the one where you're trying to escape the frigid caverns?" Jeff said.

"Dad, *no*," his son said. "This is the one where the mutated zoo animals have escaped."

"And you try to catch them?"

"They seek dominion, Dad."

"What?"

"Bam! You— Oh, no, my *boots*. What?"

"Do you catch the animals?"

"They're mutants, Dad. You shoot them with lava."

"So you're pretty good?"

"Oh, God, I hate this parking garage."

"What are you—do you have me on speakerphone?"

"That is not good."

"Who else is there?"

"That right there is the very worst one."

"What are you doing for Thanksgiving?"

"I think Mom's taking us— Crap! Uh-oh."

"Taking you where?"

"To . . . Grandma's."

"What about Christmas?"

"Shit. Gored *again*. You messed me up, Dad."

"What about Christmas?"

"Dad, I *told* you, I think we're going to Grandma's."

In the machines there were rows and rows of snacks and candy. There they were, in full sight, bright and satisfying and twenty-five percent larger. The vending alcove operated by the honor system. Jeff was bound by his honor not to tip the machine over and smash it open with his Gary Clark helmet.

THE FIGURE AT THE FAR END of the fourth-floor hallway seemed inhuman in its shape and movement. It was Myron. Chad had bestowed upon him the Rick Donnalley gear, but Myron had yet to bestow his Leonard Marshall gear upon Vince, whom he could not find. Thus Myron was one of several men who trudged a long hallway with two bulky sets of gear and a faraway look in his eyes. When he slowly emerged from silhouette, the men in their doorways could see that his face had a startled look, and that two helmets hung like decapitated heads from his hooked fingers. After some confusion and misinformation, Steven explained to the tight ends that the Gorgon was a type of monster, and that the Medusa was the name of a specific Gorgon. Also, that Perseus had beheaded Medusa, though Perseus had not beheaded Medusa in a giant maze.

And where was Fat Michael?

He was in the stairwell between the second and third floors, hiding from Peter, who was searching for him.

Why?

To give him the Theismann gear.

No, why was he hiding?

It's difficult to say.

Was it unusual for the man selected to play Theismann to hide in the stairwell?

No.

Did hiding remind Fat Michael of anything from childhood?

There was a boy he used to hide from with some frequency. The boy had a metal leg brace, and Fat Michael could always hear it creaking and thumping as the boy climbed the front porch of the foster home. He hid beneath his bed as the boy rang the doorbell.

Why did he hide?

He didn't want to see that boy.

Did Fat Michael like his nickname?

No. Would you?

How was Fat Michael passing the time in the stairwell?

He was lining up the bodies of dead ladybugs. There were nine. Then some light stretching.

Would Fat Michael have come this weekend if his missing dog had not returned late last night, smelling like garbage?

It's difficult to say.

Would Peter ever find Fat Michael?

Yes, Gil would eventually tip him off.

What would Peter say to Fat Michael?

He would say that everyone should play Theismann once. He would say it's hard to explain, but it's an intense experience. What he would mean was that it's powerful to relinquish control, particularly for those men, like Fat Michael, who are determined never to relinquish control.

Why did Peter always wear that mouthguard?

It made him feel safe.

What would Fat Michael say?

He would say not to call him that.

What else would he say?

He would ask Peter about the drought and a new operating system.

Would he apologize?

There would be no need.

Would he clack the shoulder pads with his fist?

Yes.

Would anyone else join them there?

Terence, a guy from Prestige Vista Solutions.

What would the men's voices sound like in that stairwell?

Hushed and loud at the same time.

CHAD WALKED ALONG the fourth-floor hallway. He had no shadow, and his feet made no sound as he walked. The hotel had transformed his sense of scale and reference. Chad had ceased being a discrete unit of biological meaning. It felt okay. The sound from Room 414 may or may not have been a cat.

It was not yet late, but many guests had already hung their lewd *Do Not Disturb* signs from their door handles. Chad thought of them as *Do Not Disturb* signs, though in fact they did not say *Do Not Disturb*. There were no words on the signs at all. At some point in the history of hospitality, it occurred to Chad, the *Do Not Disturb* sign had become symbolic, metaphorical. It no longer utilized the crude and literal three-word injunction that ineluctably suggested wanton acts within. These signs on the fourth floor featured a sprig of bamboo leaning evocatively against a lurid stack of polished black wellness stones. This ideograph, as it turned out, was no less prurient than the old imperative, though it was no doubt more sensual than carnal. Moving noiselessly through the hall, imagining the varieties of intercourse to his port and starboard, Chad collected the signs from the door handles as he passed.

In an attempt to avoid Andy and Nate, Chad stepped into an elevator containing Andy and Nate.

"We were just looking for you," Andy said.

"Me, too," Chad said as the doors closed.

The men were quiet as the elevator dropped slowly toward the lobby. Andy took a long, slow drink from his red cup. Nate stared at the illuminated number above the doors, confirming the descent. Chad looked down at the shoes his wife disliked so forcefully. His wife's contempt for the shoes was in fact their primary feature, more salient than their color, style, material, or comfort. He could not even see the shoes anymore. He could see only that face she made. The shoes were haunted. Why did she insist on expressing her disdain for these shoes? Or put another way, why did he continue to wear them? On the floor was a sticky note that read *45 DAYS*. Chad felt trapped. The elevator stopped on the first floor, and the men got out. Standing on the floral carpet, Chad suffered that fleeting vertiginous wobble that health experts in an Internet anxiety forum had diagnosed as either an inner ear malady or multiple sclerosis. Nate felt it, too, an unpleasant dipping sensation, his assiduously untested hypothesis having always been that the operations of the elevator create tremors and vibrations in the hallway area in the immediate vicinity of the shaft.

Without speaking or conferring in any way, the men turned and walked down the hallway toward the side exit of the hotel, and it seemed to each man that their pace slowed as they neared the door. Outside the exit, there was a picnic table next to a dumpster, and it was there that these three men traditionally convened for a post-lottery smoke. During the year, however, Chad had quit smoking, and he had yet to tell Nate and Andy. He did not know Nate and Andy well. He saw them once a year, and these nighttime smokes by the hotel dumpster were the sole basis of their friendship. They had created sub-tradition, sub-community. Chad had not quite articulated this to himself, but he felt that it would be inhospitable not to smoke at the picnic table with Andy and Nate. It would perhaps be construed as a renunciation, or as a claim of superiority or judgment. Because he saw them only one weekend per year, it might seem to them that the reason he had quit smoking was that he no longer desired their friendship, when in fact there had been other reasons that he had quit smoking cigarettes. He did not want the other men to think that he did not value their company, though in truth he valued their company only very slightly.

Nate, also, had quit smoking nine months ago, but was reluctant, obviously, to tell Chad and Andy. For Nate there was something distasteful, almost shameful, in quitting. Doctors and schoolchildren and righteous billboards were always exhorting him to quit, and even though they were right, Nate found repugnant the notion that he must capitulate. It made him feel like a child, and he hated being made to feel like a child—though he supposed that Charles would say that nobody can make you feel anything. He had wanted to quit, of course, but to quit was to obey, to be good instead of bad, and he did not want to admit to annual smoking friends that he had surrendered.

Andy had also quit smoking during the year, but he simply could not find a way to tell Chad and Nate. Andy had quit smoking numerous times in the past—in fact, a year ago when they had smoked beside the dumpster, Andy had not previously smoked in six months—and he had become sheepish about the very attempt to quit. He was reluctant to tell the other two because he did not want to see the knowing smirks, the nods, the raised eyebrows of men who very well knew he could never really quit. "Let us know how that works out for you," one of them might say. "Good luck with that," the other might say, though in fact it was difficult to imagine either Chad or Nate saying such things. The three men moved toward the exit door with lassitude and dread. They might never reach the door. A desk clerk watching the men on closed-circuit television might have thought they were demonstrating one of the paradoxes of motion, though the desk clerk was not watching the monitor but instead reading Ayn Rand's *The Fountainhead*. Each man, it is true, was also beginning to crave a cigarette.

Outside, the rain still fell, not hard but insistent, and at cruel angles. Chad's shoes became heavy and wet, but even with these new qualities they were still, primarily, the shoes that his wife disliked. The shoes had become a host for parasitic scorn. The eggs of his wife's contempt had hatched inside Chad's shoes, and now the larvae feasted on the leather uppers. The three men stood hunched by the picnic table in November. Beside them was the dumpster, brimming with sodden cardboard. Only cigarettes—only their glowing orange tips—could give meaning or coherence to this scene, and yet none of the men carried cigarettes. Thinking quickly, which is to say without thinking at all, Chad bent down to unlace his shoes.

IN THE DEFENSIVE LINEMEN'S ROOM, Vince and Carl were arguing about electrocution. Vince claimed that the volts killed you, while Carl seemed certain that it was the amps. The debate had entered a silent phase, during which each man, working intently on his laptop, rapidly sent the other man Internet links that corroborated his position. The unread links piled up in each man's in-box faster than he could delete them. Then Carl, mindlessly palpating the hard, tender lump in his armpit, began to watch a video of the demolition of the Seattle Kingdome, while Vince began to watch a video of juvenile red pandas playing in the snow.

Wesley did not feel well, and he left the room. In the vending alcove, he stepped over Peter, who was sitting on the floor with the gear of both Theismann and Kenny Hill, talking on speakerphone to a loved one whose attention was not fully on Peter. "Tell him I promise we'll do marshmallows next weekend," Peter said. Wesley assumed the vending machine would not contain ginger ale, and he was correct.

There was no sidewalk along the service road. There was, instead, a narrow dirt path through the pallid grass and litter. Wesley walked the path, ducking beneath tree limbs, his shoulders lifted against the cold rain. He did not own an umbrella. Like sunglasses or suitcases, an umbrella seemed to Wesley to be a kind of luxury item. He needed it only occasionally, which is to say he did not really need it. His stomach felt unsettled, but he enjoyed the walk. He found poignancy on the path. A sidewalk merely represented a planner's idea of where you might walk, where you should walk. A sidewalk revealed no history, no desire. It yielded few traces of its use. A sidewalk was prescriptive, dogmatic. A path, though, was the expression, the record, of something vital and communal. An individual, no matter how determined, could not create a dirt path. The path expressed and served the aspirations of many. It represented a kind of bottom-up history—no matter what anyone thought people might do, this was what people had done, what they did, they walked here, the dirt now so compact it did not turn to mud in the rain. Wesley felt connected to the thousands of people whose feet had contributed to the path, those who had walked along this ugly and perilous service road, day and night, for years. He could see his breath in the cold. He tried not to think about the year that Bald Michael got mugged. He passed a small group from Prestige Vista Solutions, exchanging with the group a nod and a stoic greeting that Wesley found moving. Beyond a high and steep embankment, the interstate ran parallel to the service road, and he could hear the cars and trucks passing at illicit velocity. The embankment was festooned with plastics that glowed wetly in the dark. By night it looked ceremonial, festive, as if it had once stood for something holy but now just stood prettily for itself. Drivers on the service road honked boisterously at Wesley, and their male passengers leaned out windows to startle him with invective. "Don't get wet, jackass!" shouted a passenger in a cowboy hat. "Homo walk!" shouted another. "Boo!" yelled a face from a sunroof. "I'm a ghost!" Though he knew it was not personal, Wesley always took this kind of spontaneous and indiscriminate meanness personally, and it demoralized him. He was a real estate lawyer for a major department store, but it did not matter, he knew. Anyone could be heckled walking a dirt path along a service road.

The terminus of the dirt path was a parking lot shared by a biscuit restaurant and a convenience store that offered the state minimum prices on cigarettes. Wesley emerged from beneath the large branch of a tree, and walked like a man presumed dead through the wet lot to the flickering brightness of the convenience store. Inside, he examined the refrigerated drinks. Just as he no longer recognized the celebrities on the covers of magazines, or the songs on contemporary radio, he did not recognize most of these brands. There was beer, there was soda, there were sports drinks, there were energy drinks, there were water drinks, and there were coffee and tea drinks. There were a lot of rockets, feathers, and glowing feline eyes. There was a lot of packaging that was made to look as though it had been shredded by fierce talons. All of these dazzling stimulants and depressants, all these water variants, but no ginger ale to settle a queasy stomach. Wesley did not want to be transformed. He did not want to be a werewolf. He wanted to be a slightly less uncomfortable version of himself. He wanted, it's true, to feel safe and loved. He could not help but remember the way that his mother would cut the toast into buttery strips. It seemed impossible to Wesley that the store did not offer ginger ale. Had his culture just given up on comfort? A culture that has moved beyond ginger ale, Wesley thought, is a culture that has moved beyond nurturance. How could such a childish culture have such contempt for childhood? Wesley stood so long in front of the drinks cooler that the cashier asked him curtly if he needed help.

"I'm just blind," Wesley said. "I can't find the ginger ale."

"Not here, man," the cashier said. "Just beer, no liquor."

Wesley knew better than to look for saltine crackers. He glanced again at the drinks, then he circled the store without picking up or purchasing anything, walking very slowly and with his hands out of his pockets, so as not to look like a shoplifter. In his attempt to allay suspicion, he aroused suspicion, and the cashier watched him carefully, one hand beneath the counter, fingers wrapped around the sticky tape of a baseball bat.

·

IN THE FRACTURE COMPOUND, Gary, Bald Michael, and George sat on beds, passing George's flask of homemade liquor. Bald Michael, grimacing and shuddering at the aftertaste, handed the flask to Gary, who grimaced and shuddered while drinking. George grimaced and shuddered in anticipation of his next drink. The small flask, which seemed never to become empty, had been a gift to George from his Wiccan coworker at the public library.

"Damn, damn, damn," Bald Michael said, shuddering.

Gary wore Taylor's two white wristbands, so bright they revealed other allegedly white objects—the men's teeth and eyes, their stretched V-neck T-shirts, the pillowcases—to be yellow or gray. The ring finger and middle finger of Gary's left hand were taped together, though not in historically accurate fashion. He dropped from the bed to the floor, and performed nineteen push-ups. When finished he lay on the floor, breathing. There were people who could do one hundred push-ups. He wished he could lose fifteen pounds. He thought of Fat Michael, that vein in his arm. It would not be satisfying to destroy, ceremonially, Fat Michael's leg. With his ear pressed to the carpet Gary thought he could hear the subterranean rumbling of the hotel's complex machinery, but he knew that didn't make sense because he was on the fifth floor. He was in a box inside a bigger box. The carpet was redolent of nothing at all. Granted one wish, Gary had chosen invincibility. It was often the case that the men who chose Taylor experienced a post-lottery affective crash that left them anxious, listless, disappointed, and sad.

And something else—perhaps frightened, or preemptively guilt-ridden. Bald Michael was talking about air quality again.

"Hey, man," George said to Gary. "You okay?"

Gary tried to nod, but the flesh of his cheek against the hotel carpet had a relatively high coefficient of static friction, and his head barely moved.

"Hey," George said, "you want me to walk on your back?"

"No," Gary said quickly, though George was already peeling off his black socks.

Nate, the fourth linebacker, entered the room. He was not wearing shoes.

"Hey, Nate," George said, "can you turn off that light? Yeah, that one."

Nate turned off the light.

"And can you put that jersey over the bedside lamp?"

Nate laughed, though he did not know why. He draped Bald Michael's Gary Reasons jersey over the lamp, and the room grew dim and blue. George unzipped his duffel bag, and selected a CD. He looked around the room, then inserted the CD into Gary's laptop on the orange chair.

Gary said, "Hey, George, I don't think—" but the first track on the mountain dulcimer compilation was "Wildwood Flower," and he found that he could not complete his objection.

"Wait until you hear 'Shady Grove,'" George said. "Gary, you're going to want to lift your shirt up."

With his face still on the carpet, Gary lifted his shirt up.

"Okay, Gary," George said. "You ready?"

Gary did not respond, and George approached with his pant legs rolled. Gary stared at George's feet, which were coarse and clean and dry, with high arches, long and hairless toes, and toenails that appeared to be trimmed but not fussily managed. The feet were not tender and pale, helpless in the way of baby animals, but neither were they the hairy, black-soled, thick-nailed feet of a wandering hippie. If they had a smell, it was faint and mild and organic, like cucumber or loam. They were good feet, expressive of proper values. Observing no overt sign of resistance, George stepped onto the middle of Gary's back. Gary grunted, winced, squeezed his eyes shut. George stood still for a moment, achieving his balance, allowing Gary to grow accustomed to the weight. "There you go," George said. "That's it. Arms straight out. Now find your breath. Find it." Gary tried to find his breath, and gradually he found it. The dulcimer played "Black Mountain Rag," and George began slowly to shift his weight from one foot to the other. In his cold, wet socks Nate watched, wincing in sympathy with Gary. He could feel George's feet on his own back. He could feel a shortness of breath. Bald Michael took several pictures of George and Gary with his phone. Eventually George began to shuffle deliberately up and down Gary's back. His balance was excellent.

"How's that?" George said.

Gary grunted and tried to nod.

"Seriously," George said, "feels like I'm standing on a coil of rope, man."

With a librarian on his back, with dulcimer music in

the air, with the cold rain still tapping the window, with the heavy mantle of Lawrence Taylor upon his shoulders, Gary had the rare opportunity to break down entirely. He felt he could really lose it, and he was startled by the energy it took to resist it. "How . . . did . . . you . . . know?" Gary said.

"About your back?"

Gary tried to nod.

"Man," George said, "it's everyone's back that hurts."

Nate was hoping he would be next, though he could not bring himself to ask. The dulcimer played "Whiskey Before Breakfast." In the dim blue light, Bald Michael looked through the photographs he had taken, deleting each one for its failure to portray.

JEFF HAD A THEORY about marriage:

All it is, he said, and he said he learned this too late, but all it is, is watching someone and having someone watch you. He paced in front of the mute television, on which a pickup truck drove over boulders in slow motion. He sounded exasperated, as if the other eligible receivers in Room 440 (Randy, Steven, and Derek) had worn him down, forced him to defend his position, though in fact no one had asked him anything, and no one had been speaking about marriage. No one had been speaking much at all. That's all it is, he said. He said when you're a kid, your parents watch your life. They know what's going on, they're watching you pretty carefully. Or at least let's hope they are. They know you have a spelling quiz or a baseball game, they keep track of it all, and so you get the idea that your life is important, valuable. But then you grow up, Jeff said, and it turns out nobody is really watching anymore. It would be weird if your parents knew that you switched cereals in the morning, or that the power went out at your office for two hours. Nobody really knows what your days are like. Jeff said he wasn't talking about the big things—moving to a new city or having a kid or losing your job. He said he was talking about the tiny, stupid crap that fills most of our days, and that you can't tell people about because it's too small and stupid. But it's your life, Jeff said, right? It doesn't matter to anyone else, he said, but it matters to you because it's your life. The water in your basement, the strange smell in your shower drain. Changing your kid's bedsheets in the middle of the night. Jeff said that life is a precious gift, sure, but usually what life is, is going to the store to buy a stupid piece of shit-ass hardware, and then buying the wrong size, and then having to go back to get the right goddamn size, except the store doesn't have it. If you're not married, Jeff said, chances are, nobody sees you make two trips to the store on Saturday morning for that hinge or flange that you don't even get. Marriage—Jeff saw it so clearly now—what marriage does is at least guarantee that one person is watching. There's one person who knows you got the oil changed today, or that you waited over an hour for your dentist appointment, or that you're trying a new shave gel, or that the running shoes you've worn for years got discontinued. On television an adopted child was reunited with her birth mother, but none of the men saw it. And here's the thing, Jeff said. The wife does not have to care about any of this stuff. It would be weird if she did, Jeff said, right? Because it's boring, he said, and because she has her own tiny crap she's got going on in her own life, and that seems important to her. And you're watching that for her, Jeff said. See? You don't have to care, he said. You just have to watch. You just have to be sentient, a witness. You don't even have to watch very carefully. You're not a scientist. You're not some astronomer. It's not like that, Jeff said. It's certainly not about keen perception, and it's not about gratitude or sympathy or even appreciation. It really is not about giving or getting credit. Just, Jeff said, just trying to keep the squirrels out of the goddamn mulch. If that person who is watching happens to love you or respect you, or if that person concedes to have oral sex with you, that's a bonus, Jeff said, but it's not necessary. It's not what marriage is for. It's just vital to have someone who sees your life. It's no small thing. And look, Jeff said to the men, if you want any more from marriage than that, you'll be disappointed. He walked to the door, squinted into the peephole. If you want to be connected, Jeff said, or if you want to share a passion, or if you're thinking *at all* in terms of big, old trees with thick roots, you're going to end up on the couch. First the couch, he said, then a crappy studio apartment. The only thing marriage can really give you is the sense that your life is witnessed by another person. A kind of validation, Jeff said. That's it, he said, and it's plenty. If you have that, you have a lot. You have everything. But here's the thing, Jeff said. People don't like being watched. They resent it. Jeff said that he resented it. He said he wanted to be free from it. He wanted his wife to mind her own business. But when he got away from it—when his wife was no longer watching—he didn't feel free, he said. He didn't feel relieved or liberated. He didn't. He said now he just feels like there's suddenly no point at all to buying the wrong kind of caulk for the windows. You're not in a movie, Jeff said. He said that over and over. Nobody sees you, he said. He said that's why people pretend they're in movies. People say they want privacy, but they would actually like a camera out in their cold backyard at midnight, pointed through the kitchen window while they make a school lunch for their kids. They want someone to just notice, Jeff said. He said that's what marriage is for. Otherwise, he said, honest to God, we're all just like penguins at the North Pole, doing it all for no real reason.

Steven stood at the window, listening to the dark rain. Any weather, when sustained, begins to feel like an interrogation technique. He needed to call the front desk to report the theft of the lottery drum. He needed to tell Randy that Donnie Warren's wrists are wrapped in tape. It looks like wristbands, but it's not. It's tape. Was Jeff still talking about marriage? Was he still yammering with his stupid face about squirrels digging up the mulch? Steven didn't care at all about anything Jeff said. Steven would rather hash things out with *George* than endure another speech from Jeff about human relationships. For some reason he found the mention of astronomy particularly infuriating. He checked his phone for pictures or news from the school play, but there was nothing. He was, of course, still glad he had come. He could not have not come.

Randy lay on the bed, flipping through a woodworking catalogue. He disliked Jeff, but not strongly, so he was free to ignore him. Derek lay beside Randy, bored and restless. He was not listening to Jeff. What if, Derek had been wondering, the offense just didn't run the Throwback Special? What if they drew up another play in the dirt? What if they broke the huddle and then surprised the defense with some other play? They could change the snap, even go with a silent count. Why had this never occurred to him before? Was it crazy? Steven would never go along with it. Randy would. It was an insidious thought, and drunken. A draw is particularly effective against aggressive linebackers, Derek considered. Or a screen.

ADAM STOOD LOOKING out the window of Room 212 like a homesteader during an April blizzard. The defensive backs, and particularly the safeties, were the least prominent of the players. They backpedaled from tragedy, like inverse first responders. Their job was essential, but remote and untelevised. This feeling, of being important but unrecognized, distant from the hub, was all too familiar to most of the men. The long-standing notion was that the defensive backs' room was the party room—"Vegas"— but the truth was that the room typically had a sour mood and an early bedtime.

"If you work in the automotive industry, you have to be thinking about the end of cars," Adam said, still facing the window. "If you work in phones, you have to be preparing for the day when people don't use phones anymore. If you work in laptops, you spend your days imagining what comes after laptops. Everything thriving is dying. Every industry has become the fashion industry. The car is dead, the book is dead, the PC is dead. My office is paperless. *Potatoes* are somehow bad for you. People don't want to live in *houses* anymore. It's exhausting."

"Why were you so late, Adam?" Peter said.

"It was a domestic situation," Adam said.

"What isn't?" Peter said.

"It was a family emergency," Adam said.

"You got that right," Peter said.

The heating and cooling unit ticked and clanked. Chad sat in the orange chair, looking at his phone. His feet, in socks, were wet and cold. He felt that the cold, wet socks were emblematic of his folly and weakness. His throat burned from the cigarette he had bummed off that gray-faced marketer from Prestige Vista Solutions. He wished he had not smoked that cigarette. And it had been foolish to throw his shoes in the dumpster, he now realized.

The only other shoes he had were his cleats. At the time he had thrown his shoes in the dumpster he had felt a rush of defiance, but whom, exactly, had he defied? He liked the shoes, or had at one time, and so he had apparently defied only himself. He had spited his face. He had hoisted himself. His wife hated the shoes, and though she had not demanded or even suggested (nor would she, ever) that he discard the shoes, in discarding them he was, he now felt, executing remotely her unspoken wish. That the actualization of his wife's desire had felt, out in the rain by the hotel dumpster, so authentically like the actualization of his own desire, meant either that they were soul mates, or that he lived under a totalitarian regime. How was it that he could not, here in his cold, wet socks, make any meaningful distinction between compliance and defiance, or ascertain to whom he had stuck it, if indeed he had stuck it to someone? It was true, however, that his wife was frugal, and she would no doubt object to his throwing away perfectly functional (though detestable) shoes, and so in this way perhaps the act was defiant in its profligacy, like the Boston Tea Party. He would teach her a lesson. He would show her not to not like his things. But that was not what he wanted! He wanted her to like his things, which meant that inevitably she would not like some things. He cared about what she thought. If your defiance reveals vulnerability, not strength, it's really not very effective defiance. Chad's original embarrassment about buying the shoes was now compounded by the embarrassment about throwing them away. He had acted like a maniac, and now he wanted his shoes. A genuinely defiant act, he realized, would be to retrieve the shoes from the wet dumpster. That would be a bold expression of his life force. He could dry them with the hair dryer attached to the wall in the hotel bathroom. But what about Andy and Nate? They had thrown their shoes in the dumpster, too, in a spirit of inebriated and defiant camaraderie, and as an expression of their individual wills. They had all thrown their shoes away, together, instead of smoking a cigarette, but then the guy from Prestige Vista Solutions shuffled out of the side exit with a full pack, and they had all smoked a cigarette anyway, even though they had all quit. Chad *hated himself*. If he pulled his shoes out of the dumpster, Nate and Andy would no doubt see the shoes tomorrow, and they would consider the recovery a sign of weakness, not strength—a kind of capitulation to the overwhelming forces of (feminized) convention, a disavowal of their defiant ritual in the rain. Chad was trapped between two incommensurable systems of meaning. Sifting through the cold and soaking trash of the hotel dumpster would be both noble and craven, depending upon the interpretive community. "Fun here," Chad texted to his wife. "Luv u." Charles, who was either a psychologist or a psychiatrist, was here, in this room, and perhaps he could be of help to Chad, but he was at the moment occupied by Peter, who was troubled by a recent incident in the home.

(Chad had missed some of the story, but it seems that Peter had been roasting marshmallows *by himself* with his *gas stove* in the *middle of the night* when his seven-year-old son entered the kitchen and witnessed the scene. I thought I smelled something, the child had said, staring at Peter warily, refusing to return to bed. Peter just stood there with two perfectly golden marshmallows on the end of a barbecue fork. Big deal, Adam said, still staring out the window. Continue, Charles said. He had the look of one betrayed, Peter said. I think he had a hard time with it, with the idea that this person he loved and trusted could roast marshmallows while he slept. It's been a couple of weeks, and he's had trouble falling asleep. He's wet the bed a couple of times. I shouldn't have done it, I guess, Peter said. It wasn't a dessert night. A phone vibrated in a duffel bag. *I'm glad you're here, Charles. Charles, I'm glad you're here.* Chad waited in his wet socks, and the waiting felt emblematic.)

"WHERE'S ANDY?" Gil said in the offensive linemen's room.

"Probably out smoking," Trent said.

"No, he quit," Gil said.

"I could smell it on him earlier," Trent said.

Trent was lying on his back in bed. The laptop quivered on his stomach like a dog on a roof. Gil stood in front of the television, flipping rapidly through channels.

"What are you looking for?" Trent said.

"What?" Gil said.

"What show are you looking for?"

"I don't watch shows."

"Then what do you watch?"

"I don't care about individual programs," Gil said. "That kind of vertical viewing doesn't interest me."

"What interests you?"

"This," Gil said, continuing to cycle swiftly through the channels. "Holistic viewing."

"I watch shows," Trent said.

"Every channel, every show, is just part of one big show. Like every channel is a pixel, making up a larger picture, the big picture. I started watching like this, and I realized I was getting more and not really losing anything."

"What does your wife think?" Trent said.

"She hides the remote," Gil said. "But she's not a horizontal processor. She doesn't think that way. A lot of women don't."

"What about, like, cohesion?" Trent said. "Or suspense?"

"Suspense is an ancient value," Gil said.

"Exactly," Trent said. He steadied his wobbling laptop, and sent a message to the Fracture Compound about Gil's horizontal viewing.

"I had an idea to program my remote to do it for me," Gil said. "But then I realized I was thinking about it all wrong. Why alter the auxiliary technology when you could alter the primary technology? The ideal thing would be to have a dedicated channel, a station, that moved through all other channels at random. Horizon TV, I call it. I bet you could sell plenty of ad time because a thirty-second spot would seem, in contrast, like a vast narrative space.

And you'd basically have zero production and development costs. No writers, no producers, no actors. But I couldn't see a way to get past the lawyers."

Trent chuckled, staring into his screen. "Hey, Gil," he said, "I've got a mole in the Compound. Looks like George is walking on backs."

"Oh, Jesus," Gil said, rolling his eyes, though his own back had been walked on by George four years earlier, which had nearly precipitated a severe late-night breakdown. He remembered George's feet clearly, the high arches. He remembered the weight, the struggle to find his breath. He kept flipping channels, but he wasn't getting anywhere. He couldn't concentrate, and totality was eluding him. He turned off the TV and pitched the remote onto the empty bed. Pitching a remote onto a large bed was a satisfying hotel activity, and Gil retrieved the remote so that he could do it once more.

"You know, here we are, the offensive line," he said. "We're paid to do one thing, protect the quarterback."

"It was 1985," Trent said. "So we aren't paid all that much."

"Counting Warren, there are six of us down linemen, right? And five of them coming on defense? There's one thing we have to do, and we will just fail so bad at it."

"Not you," Trent said. "May is solid. Wait until you see the film."

"But six against five."

"The play call was terrible," Trent said. "I don't care what anybody says."

"It's a bad feeling, though," Gil said. "Can you even imagine what those real guys must have been feeling like the night before?"

"They didn't know it was going to happen, Gil."

"But still," Gil said.

"Hey, Gil," Trent said, chuckling at his laptop screen. "George has got his magic flask out."

Andy was gone, and Robert was in the bathroom, washing his hands and face. The bathroom fan obscured Gil's infuriating television habits, to which Robert had been introduced in a previous year. He dried off with a thin towel, noticing as he often did the twin scars on the backs of his hands. He had received both injuries as a child. One was from a cigarette, one from hot coffee. As a child—seven years old, or eight—he liked to crawl beneath chairs and tables, particularly tables draped with table-cloths. He liked to be near his family but not with them. He liked the secrecy, the privacy. His parents were always telling him to get out from under there or he would get hurt. And that's what had happened. His father dangled an after-dinner cigarette beside his chair, and the glowing tip pressed into the center of Robert's hand. At some other point, perhaps a year later, he crawled out from beneath a table he had been told not to crawl beneath, jostling the leg and spilling a mug of hot coffee onto his other hand. It had been Robert's fault, both times. His parents had not been cruel or punitive, but it was clear that they regarded the injuries as the child's fault. They felt bad for Robert, and they cared for his wounds, but they did not feel culpable. After all, they had told him repeatedly not to crawl beneath things, and they had told him what would likely happen if he did. He did not listen, and it happened just as they said it would. And that was how Robert had always thought of the injuries, too. The scars were reminders of foolish things he had done. They *stood for* his folly and mischief. The accidents happened to occur during a generation when children could be at fault, and that era was long gone. If Robert's hot coffee spilled onto his daughter, or worse, if he smoked cigarettes in the house and if one of his cigarettes burned the girl, he would clearly bear the burden of guilt and responsibility, regardless of whether he had warned her. The child's scar would stand for his carelessness, his neglect. It's not simply that he would feel it as censure from others (though he most certainly would); he would legitimately feel at fault. The child, doing childlike things, would be innocent. If you have children, you just don't dare drink hot beverages. And if you are irresponsible enough to drink hot beverages, you don't use an open-mouth mug, and you certainly don't set the mug on a table, where it could be knocked to the floor, scalding your unsuspecting child, who is merely exploring her world in a trusting, innocent, curious way (their brains are like sponges!), and who could not be expected to heed admonitions in simple English to stay out from beneath the table. Robert could hold both verdicts in his mind—that his childhood injuries had been his own fault for crawling beneath a table he had been told not to crawl beneath, and that his own child's heartbreaking (and hypothetical) burn injury beneath the table would also be his fault. Neither conclusion seemed to impinge on the other, a paradox rooted either in psychology or culture. Robert did not know which. There was no point in talking to Charles because he was never any help, and in fact he seemed uninterested.

Robert left the bathroom, and nearly bumped into Andy, who was just returning to the hotel room.

"Hi, Robert," Andy said.

"Hi, Andy," Robert said. He had always liked Andy, and he was not displeased to see him. Given the alternatives, he hoped they would be sharing a bed.

"Are you done in there?" Andy said.

"It's all yours."

Holding a pair of dripping shoes, Andy entered the bathroom, closed the door, and turned on the hair dryer attached to the wall.

FAT MICHAEL was not in the touchers' room. Carrying a bottle of Advanced Water, a pack of antibacterial wipes, and his Theismann helmet, he had left the room without saying anything to Tommy and Myron. Tommy and Myron, though, could pretty well guess where he had gone.

The room, after the lottery, looked like a site of explosive violence. Pizza sauce streaked the walls, congealed bits of flesh-colored pizza lay strewn on the beds. The keg lay on its side, as if, once depleted of beer, it had perished. Having never seemed alive, it now resembled nothing so much as something dead. Crumpled napkins covered the floor like peach blossoms after the Battle of Shiloh. Tommy began to clean immediately, before Myron had an opportunity to ask or exhort him to clean. Tommy did not mind work, but he disliked being asked or told to work. If Myron had said to Tommy, "Let's get this place cleaned up," Tommy would have immediately become sullen and insolent, but if he could begin on his own initiative, he could labor assiduously. Myron, who also did not like to be asked or told to do work, immediately left the room to get a trash can before Tommy could ask him to go find a trash can. He found one in the vending alcove, which clicked and hummed. He had to step over the legs of a man from Prestige Vista Solutions, who sat on the floor, chanting lifelessly into his phone, "But *that* does *not* make *any* sense." Myron filled the trash can while Tommy scrubbed the walls with a white washcloth that almost instantly turned pink. The activities began as a kind of race, but each man slowed as he realized that the race's winner would be forced to clean the bathroom, an unpleasant task. The problem with doing your work fast was that you made more work for yourself. Myron finished first, but then left the room with his trash can, staying gone, Tommy thought, for a suspiciously long time. Tommy draped the keg with a towel, then trudged alone into the bathroom.

Later, their space tidy if not dry or fragrant, Tommy and Myron sat in chairs on opposite sides of the room, throwing a football and talking about public education. Myron's kids' school's library's roof had collapsed under the weight of snow last winter. Tommy's kid's teacher's aide was someone he could not stop thinking about. Because he called her "striking" and "pretty," because he talked about her "features" and her "figure," Tommy did not sound creepy to Myron, nor to himself. It was but a partial and genteel confession of his depravity, and it trailed off into silence and obscene ideation. The men did not need to talk because they were throwing and catching a football. Or, if they chose, they could talk about throwing and catching a football. Eventually, of course, one man sat beneath the window and tried to time his throw so that the other man, running from the door, could make a diving catch on the queen bed. They alternated positions. Both men became flushed and sweaty. Neither man cared to remember the year that Vince broke the corner off of a bedside table. Both went about the game with gravity and good-natured intensity. It was important to them to throw and catch the ball well.

"Nice one."

"My fault, bad throw."

"The one-handed grab!"

"I suck."

"That one will no doubt be reviewed."

"I used to be able to do that."

"Lead me a little more next time."

"Crap."

"Whoa."

"You okay?"

"Nice one."

"Got my bell rung."

"Hold on."

"Broke the plane!"

"It went in the closet, I think."

"Fearless over the middle."

"I have to blow my nose."

"That's it."

"On a roll now."

"Oh, shit."

"That was my bad."

The wall sconce was chipped, but functional. The men quit their game, and prepared for bed. They texted their wives, brushed their teeth. Fat Michael had still not returned. Tommy and Myron got into the same queen-size bed. Myron asked Tommy if he wanted to read, and they both laughed. Myron turned off the light. Tommy, it seemed to Myron, fell asleep immediately. He had never seen someone fall asleep so quickly.

In the faint red glow of the alarm clock, Myron could see the empty bed they had left for Fat Michael. It was customary for the man playing Theismann to sleep alone. It was intended to be a perk, or a compensation, but it had always seemed to Myron to be mildly punitive, a form of exile or symbolic estrangement. Myron, who six or seven years ago had been Theismann, imagined Fat Michael slipping into bed later tonight. He knew what it was like. Now Myron, feeling Tommy's warmth beside him, remembered so very clearly that time after the birth of his first child. He remembered tucking her in at night, leaving her alone in the dark of her room. It had always seemed odd to him, somehow unfair or backward, that the adults could sleep together at night for warmth and comfort, while the child, fearful and lonely, had to sleep by herself.

IN BED, in the dark, Andy and Robert talked quietly about injuries. Robert's neighbor had sliced himself wickedly with a hedge trimmer. There had been blood on the *roof*. Andy knew it didn't sound like much, but he had ended up in the ER because of a splinter from his back deck. Both men had been laid out with back spasms. Both men found themselves using the railing when they climbed stairs. Neither man could put on socks while standing up. They had both lived in the paradise of a painless body for years without even realizing it. The inglorious body had become, for Robert and Andy, one of life's most prominent themes. They often woke up sore, scanning their minds for possible causes. Each man in the bed cupped his genitals, not for arousal but for comfort.

"I'm sorry to hear about your marriage," Robert didn't say.

"It's just one of those things," Andy didn't respond. Nor did he say anything about the day he and his wife told their two children. That night, one of his final nights in the house, Andy went to check on his nine-year-old son in his room. He planned to sit on the edge of the boy's bed, to say things to him while he slept. But the boy wasn't there. Andy searched the house, gripping his phone, preparing to call someone, the police. Finally, he climbed to the third floor to his thirteen-year-old daughter's bedroom. Andy said none of this to Robert. He opened his daughter's bedroom door gently, even though he was expressly not allowed in the room, and had not been for a couple of years. A lamp was on inside. Andy smelled the fresh paint. She had painted her walls. The color was ridiculous, but she had done a neat job. The room was heartbreakingly clean and organized. The items on her bookshelves were arranged perfectly. He had had no idea what was up here, but he never would have guessed this. A silk butterfly dangled from the ceiling, spinning slowly in an invisible draft. The girl was in bed, texting. Andy's son was curled beside her, asleep. His son and daughter didn't even like each other. All they did was fight. The boy was not allowed in this room. Andy's daughter did not look up from her phone. Andy nodded to her, and he left the room.

Robert knew that Andy was going through a hard time. He knew he had a kid, maybe two. The question Robert would not ask had a long answer that Andy would not provide. Robert wanted to help. He wanted to give something to Andy. "My mother has Alzheimer's," he said quietly.

"Really?" Andy said. "Robert, I'm sorry to hear that."

"Thanks," Robert said.

This was something Robert could offer, even if it wasn't true. He had just visited his mother in Wisconsin, and though her mind certainly was not as sharp as it had once been, she was doing just fine, still living by herself. Together they had handed out candy to neighborhood trick-or-treaters. They had run out of treats and turned the porch light out at eight o'clock. Then they had watched a documentary about the enormous salt mines beneath the Great Lakes.

- 4 -

THE FOUNTAIN

THE EMPTY HALLWAYS WERE HAZY WITH sconce light and Wi-Fi radio waves. The small red lights of ceiling smoke detectors blinked in no discernible pattern. An elevator car rumbled in its shaft, transporting nothing but a name tag (*Marc*) and the scent of degraded deodorant. A ghost coursed the stairwell. The vending alcoves clicked and hummed.

Vince's T-shirt read *Daytona Beach*, and he snored intermittently.

Carl's T-shirt read *No Coffee No Peace*, and the Sharpie wouldn't wash off his hands.

Wesley's T-shirt read *Richardson's Lawn & Garden*, and he composed, in his mind, in the dark, a long letter to his son.

Gary's tank top read *I ATE THE MEGABURGER*, and he snored aggressively.

Bald Michael's T-shirt read *Miller High Life*, and his sleep apnea machine made a pleasant bubbling sound like a fish tank.

George's T-shirt had a picture of Darwin with an enormous block of text far too small to read, and he snored slowly.

Nate's T-shirt read *WTF?*, and in the dark he regretted the cigarette.

Robert's T-shirt was inside out to conceal the design, and in the dark he worried that his older daughter was developing an eating disorder.

Andy's T-shirt read *Which Way to Rock City?*, and he snored like a cartoon hound.

Gil's T-shirt had a picture of Thor and Loki, and his hand was asleep beneath his pillow.

Myron's T-shirt was yellow, and he snored with a placid countenance.

Tommy's T-shirt was incomprehensible, and he snored beneath his mustache.

Fat Michael's sweaty shirt read *Bailey's Peak Challenge 2006*, and he ran seven-minute miles on the treadmill in the hotel's Workout Center, wearing his Joe Theismann helmet and staring blankly over the single bar of the face mask into the wall-length mirror.

Derek's T-shirt read *University of Virginia School of Law*, and in the dark he wondered if he should put some pachysandra or other ground cover on that steep slope in his backyard.

Steven's T-shirt had a picture of sunlight passing through a prism, and he snored consistently.

Jeff's T-shirt read *Ninja in Training*, and he told Steven, snoring beside him, that as much as he hated to say it, this would probably have to be his last year.

Randy's T-shirt read *Thompson Optical*, and he could begin to feel the gentle tug of the pill.

Chad's T-shirt read *California Dreamin'*, and he snored without making a sound.

Charles's V-neck T-shirt was white, and all of his T-shirts were V-neck and white.

Adam's T-shirt read *Second Place Is the First Loser*, and in the dark he calculated his chances.

Peter's T-shirt was blue, and he stared at the clock, waiting for the number to change.

Trent's T-shirt read *Big Data*, and although he courteously wore a nasal strip, he snored with calamitous volume. When he woke up, he discovered that his nose was running. Though he did not have a cold, or he hadn't had a cold when he went to bed, mucus was now streaming down his face, his neck. In the dark he reached toward the bedside table for a tissue or towel. He grasped something soft, and brought it to his face. As he did so, he realized that the mucus was blood, and that the tissue was a jersey.

In the bathroom, with the light on and the door closed, Trent stopped the nosebleed by clogging his nostrils with bits of toilet paper. He unwadded Gil's Mark May jersey and held it up in front of the mirror. The stain was intense, and extensive. With despair, Trent considered (reasonably, but incorrectly) that this year might now very well be remembered primarily as the year that Trent ruined Gil's jersey, instead of the year that Randy picked Donnie Warren seventh in the lottery, or the year that Adam came late, or the year of the weird pizza guy, or the year without the conference room, or the year of Tommy's mustache. Trent could not remember the edict about laundering bloodstains, whether it involved cold water or hot water or club soda or what. In the dark room he found his pants. His belt jingled like a sleigh on the eaves. Someone in the room was snoring like a lazy dog in a cartoon. He eased the door shut, walked toward the elevator with bare feet and a bloody jersey. Angela, one of the more than a dozen vice presidents in the top-heavy management structure of Prestige Vista Solutions, watched Trent from the peephole of Room 318, and then called the front desk.

Trent waited by the elevator, but it did not arrive. A door led to the stairwell. Trent closed his eyes and extended his index finger, touching lightly the Braille letters on the sign beside the door. Repeatedly he moved his finger left to right across the tiny raised dots. *Stairs*, he said to himself. *Stairs*. When he opened his eyes, he saw that he was reading not Braille letters but the knobby residue of pink gum on the wall. Astonished, he put his fingers back on the letters.

He walked down the stairs, keeping his eyes closed. He could feel the layers of paint on the railing. He could hear the rain, the service road villainy, the metronomic beat of Fat Michael's stride on the treadmill in the Workout Center. Through occluded nostrils he smelled chlorine, though the hotel did not have an indoor pool. He put two feet on each step, a blind and barefoot man clutching a bloody jersey. After descending two flights, Trent opened his eyes. He looked first at the bottoms of his feet, then wished he hadn't. He saw a door marked *Lobby*, and he saw the stairs continue down. His eyes now open, he walked slowly down the stairs another flight to a door marked *Staff Only*. Propped beside the door at the bottom of the dim stairwell was a wet bicycle with a basket attached to its handlebars. In the basket, a glistening bike helmet and a thermos. Trent laid the jersey across the bicycle seat. He unscrewed the two lids of the thermos, and put his face to the opening. It was vegetable soup! The steam from the hot soup washed his skin, and he drew the vapor through his mouth, deep into his lungs. He screwed on the lids, returned the thermos to the basket, and removed the jersey from the bicycle seat.

Beyond the door marked *Staff Only* was a long, dark hallway, lined with locked doors of supply rooms and offices—manager, assistant manager, head of housekeeping, head of maintenance, and someone named Mr. Cottrell, on whose door was affixed a yellowed quotation by George Bernard Shaw: "The great advantage of a hotel is that it is a refuge from home life." On the cinder-block wall a bulletin board featured the grainy mug shots of recent employees of the month. At the end of the hallway, Trent found a door labeled *Laundry*, and he went inside. The laundry room was large, loud, bright, and blurry with heat. An entire wall was lined with enormous washing machines and dryers, all in use, humming and spinning and vibrating. Another wall was lined floor-to-ceiling with shelves containing sheets, pillowcases, and towels, folded and stacked. The smell in the room, not unpleasant, was as if the towels and linens had been slightly singed. In the corner, a large birdcage, draped with a dark T-shirt, was suspended by a yellow rope from the ceiling. Trent stood blinking in the white heat. He looked down at his jersey. The stain was the reddest thing he had ever seen. In the heat and the light he was suddenly aware of his own substantial weight, the burdensome layers of himself.

In a corner next to the washing machines Trent saw an enormous pile of jumbled sheets, five or six feet high, presumably dirty, though spotless and white. Trent took three steps toward the pile, and noticed that it was concave across the top like a bowl or a nest, and inside the pile of linens he saw dark clothes against the white. He stepped closer and looked in. There he saw a man and a woman, both wearing hotel uniforms. They were lying on their backs, holding hands, asleep. Trent checked for their breath, watched their chests rise and fall. Their faces were flushed in the heat. The woman was perhaps thirty. The name tag on her vest read *Holly*. The man was a bit older, with streaks of gray in his dark hair. He did not have a name tag on his vest. Their breathing was synchronized, their fingers interlaced. Later, Trent's wife would ask him if the man and woman were wearing wedding rings, but it had not occurred to Trent to look for rings, and he would not remember. Holly appeared to be pregnant, though Trent could not be sure. He knew that pregnant women should not sleep on their backs—it restricts blood flow to the fetus—and yet he also knew how important sleep was during pregnancy.

Trent heard a scuffling sound behind the T-shirt draped over the birdcage. He backed away from the nest of sheets, as you back away from royalty. At the door, he turned and left the room, making sure the heavy door closed without a sound. He walked through the dark hallway and into the stairwell, which still smelled of soup. He climbed the stairs to the lobby. There, directly before him, in the center of the lobby, the celebrated fountain was burbling and splashing, its series of bowls filling and spilling merrily. The yellow tape had been removed, as had the notice from the health department. The fountain was large, though not ostentatious. It was, as the Internet reviews claimed, an attractive feature, and a visitor admiring the centerpiece of the lobby would never have guessed that he currently stood one hundred yards from a roaring interstate with floral crosses in its median. There was a woman on her knees in front of the fountain, her back to Trent. She had removed her shoes and placed them tidily on the floor beside her. When Trent approached, he saw that her long sleeves were rolled, her elbows resting on the edge of the fountain. She gripped a toothbrush, and she diligently scrubbed a light stain on a white blouse.

The woman did not look up at Trent as he neared the fountain. "An old traveler's trick," she said, scrubbing.

Trent nodded, though he didn't understand.

"They put so much bleach in," she said.

Trent looked around. He could see, through the automatic doors, a luggage cart gleaming in the rain. At the front desk, a young clerk stared at a monitor. He paid no attention to Trent or to the woman.

"He doesn't care?" Trent asked, pointing at the desk clerk.

"He doesn't see," she said.

Trent knelt beside the woman, exposing the dirty soles of his feet to security cameras. He looked up at the young clerk, but he was no longer visible behind the desk and monitor. With great effort he resisted looking at the enormous clock, as he did not want a way to name the moment. He did not know if it was early or late. The television in the lobby was, remarkably, off.

"Do you mind?" he asked.

She shook her head. "The fountain is for everyone," she said. Her tone was inaccessible to Trent. The sentence was a locked pine box, simple and pretty. She looked at Trent for the first time. She smiled, deepening the mystery. As she turned back to her work, Trent realized for the first time that he was still wearing his nasal strip, that his nostrils were still clogged with red bits of toilet paper.

"Help yourself," she said, indicating her toothbrush and washcloths.

Trent looked into the fountain. All of the dirty coins were gone. What would he wish for with one wish? He watched the business traveler at work beside him. The muscles of her forearm fluttered as she scrubbed. Wispy strands of hair pulled out of her ponytail, dropped like a curtain in front of her face. Her necklace, some pendant or charm on a silver chain, dangled just above the water.

She was meticulous, devout in her attention. If she noticed the large bloodstain on Trent's garment, she made no indication. Trent dipped the Mark May jersey into the water of the fountain. Kneeling, silent, he tamped, brushed, and blotted the stain, imitating his fellow pilgrim. They worked together, apart. The water gurgled and splashed, cold drops leaped to touch his cheeks and neck. Gradually, the blood swam in wavy lines away from the jersey, vanishing in the clear pool.

- 5 -
RITES

I T WOULD BE DIFFICULT TO OVERSTATE THE men's enthusiasm for continental breakfast. To be clear, their zeal had little or nothing to do with this particular hotel's version of the standard spread. As petulant online reviewers made very clear, the hotel's breakfast was not in any way exceptional or distinctive. It was a completely average continental breakfast, and this was why the men loved it. The breakfast involved no surprises and no risks. It involved no deliberation and no ordering, no indecision or regret. With plastic tongs they heaped large quantities of known sweet rations onto their Styrofoam plates. Everything tasted like it looked. There were no interesting spices or herbs, no local flavors, no subtle variations on classics. It was a bounty of carbohydrates, and the items never ran out. There was always more, and it was always free. Continental breakfast made them feel—made many of them feel—as if they were getting away with something. And at the same time they felt it was a form of recognition, and at the same time they felt it was but a tiny portion of what they were owed. And so it was that the long table of processed food and crop-dusted fruit was for the men simultaneously gift, reward, and restitution. Their appetites were severe.

Wearing their jerseys, the men arrived in the dining area early, but they discovered that the buffet had been set upon by dozens of employees of Prestige Vista Solutions. The men lurked at the boundaries of the dining area, anxious about resources. They watched the employees scoop and tong and toast. The female employees decimated the fruit. The male employees leaned close to inspect the plates of pastries, their ties grazing the glaze. There was good-natured joking about PowerPoint, about the taking of minutes. Those in line for the waffle maker shared wedding photos, baby photos, house photos, injury photos. Someone had adopted three more dogs. Everyone was eager to talk to Jim—Cyber Jim, not Khakis Jim—about their computer problems. When the employees of Prestige Vista Solutions had filled their plates and cups, they filed out of the dining area, and disappeared into the conference room like a line of ants. The men in their jerseys watched, and when they turned back to the continental banquet, the serving platters had been replenished, the yogurt pyramids reconstructed. They descended on the simple sugars, ravenous but with a clear and disheartening sense that there was no real connection between breakfast and merit.

•

FAT MICHAEL stirred gray powder into each of the three plastic cups in front of him. The powder did not dissolve. In wet, floating clumps it spun inside the rims of the cups, suggesting, somehow, the passage of time. Fat Michael drank all of the cups rapidly, one after another, his eyes pinched shut. He did not look good. He looked incredible, but he did not look good. Also, he was itchy, and he raked his legs with his fingernails. Myron and Tommy sat across from Fat Michael, eating silently. It was the one time during the year they used flavored coffee creamer. Their presence at the table somehow made Fat Michael seem more alone than he would have seemed if he had actually been alone.

"This muffin is all right," Myron said in a low voice. Tommy's face looked weird because he was doing exercises to strengthen his pelvic floor.

A hotel employee named Nick walked into the dining area wearing Chad's shoes. The shoes were too small, and very wet, but he liked them. They made him feel like a lucky person, though he knew himself to be an unlucky person. He wrapped a bagel in a napkin, filled a cup with orange juice. He remembered the time when Lawrence Taylor snapped Joe Theismann's leg on *Monday Night Football*. He remembered exactly where he was, and what he was doing. He clearly remembered Howard Cosell's anguished reaction, though he remembered it incorrectly because Cosell's last season on *Monday Night Football* had been 1983. He moved toward the men in the jerseys. He had a burden he was eager to set down.

From across the room Charles saw Nick approaching the defensive backs' breakfast table with an expression of fullness, and he stood quickly, placing his napkin on the table. "Excuse me, guys," he said. He walked through the dining area, into the lobby. For a moment he stood before the fountain, which was once again dry. Each year in this hotel lobby he was forced to recall that as a child he had stolen quarters from a mall fountain (soaking the cuffs of his sweatshirt) so that he could purchase, in the filthy bathroom of a gas station near his house, an erotic puzzle entitled Boobs Galore. The small puzzle box contained nine cardboard squares that could be arranged, on a floor behind a locked bedroom door, to form a picture of a sad, shirtless woman with enormous breasts. Charles remembered that the woman, when reconstituted, was sitting on what he now knew to be a Windsor chair, and that any adolescent lust he could gin up at the sight of her demoralizingly large breasts was almost immediately dowsed by the way she looked back at Charles. The puzzle piece with her face (top row, middle column) countervailed all of the other eight pieces. That face was more nude by far than her body. The look on her face implicated Charles. It suggested that she was forced to share Charles's shame and disappointment, and she was resentful. Or perhaps Charles was forced to share her shame and disappointment, and he was resentful. In either case, Charles and this nine-piece shirtless woman in a Windsor chair had been trapped together in a sticky web of shame, disappointment, and resentment. Charles had stolen coins for this experience. In his backyard he had dug a small hole. He had put the puzzle in the hole, and then lit it with a long wooden match. It burned in blues and greens.

The young woman at the front desk was likely not aware of Charles's memory of the puzzle, though she had grown up with two older brothers. She smiled and nodded at Charles—or at a spot just above his shoulder—as he walked past the desk. "Good morning, sir," she said. Charles walked outside to verify briefly the wetness and coldness of the rain. He walked back through the automatic doors into the lobby, into the men's restroom. The restroom was empty and glistening. A stalactiform mass depended from the ceiling, dripping slowly. Charles selected a corner stall beneath a flickering fluorescent light, and he saw at once the work of the diligent vandal. Someone (Carl) had traced his left hand dozens of times. The hands filled the wall. Charles placed his left hand inside the outline of the vandal's hand. He reached high for another. The effect of the multiplicity of hands was not of many people, but of a single person amplified by trouble. Charles worked with adolescents with eating disorders, and so he knew very well the forms of desperate assertion.

THROUGH THE WINDOWS of the dining area, the hotel parking lot shone darkly in the cold rain. The lights above the lot were on, casting a weak yellow glow in the mist. At the offensive linemen's table, Gil spoke of the tiny hinges of a dollhouse roof. His Mark May jersey was radiant against the dun breads of breakfast. At a nearby table, the conversation drifted inevitably toward vasectomy and time share. Wesley said they could now cauterize the vas deferens in a scalpel-free procedure. Gary was adamant about an A-frame chalet in the Smokies. Vince heard the men out, nodding, but he said he was just not ready. "Suit yourself," Gary said, leaving the table for more instant oatmeal.

Later, full, the men pulled their chairs away from their breakfast tables. They had nowhere to be until ten o'clock. They sat, leaned back, crossed their legs at the ankles, at the knees. They drank coffee, picked at pastries. They talked, read complimentary newspapers, played games on phones, took photographs of themselves, stared at the mute television. One man worked a crossword, another put new laces in his cleats, another used the sharp edge of a business card to remove food from his teeth. Another performed a magic trick with a quarter and upside-down cups. George did chair yoga. Like the dog that licks its testicles, they refilled their coffee cups because they could. The coffee was bad, but its poor quality served to strengthen the community. The day was in front of them. The dining area, seen as a whole, appeared to be a site both of great torpor and great vitality, as the sheer variety of indolence manifested as an energetic bustle.

If asked to specify the best part of the weekend, not

one of the men would think to name this languorous interlude in the dining area, and yet there was no time better than this. This was the best time, this brief span of Saturday morning. It was not an event, could not be named or considered. Consequently, the men could enjoy it without pressure, anxiety, or self-consciousness. Indeed, without awareness. They could enjoy it without enjoying it. If they were aware of it as a potentially enjoyable event—Post-Breakfast Relaxation, 9:15–10:00, Dining Area—then it would almost certainly cease to be such an enjoyable event. Disappointment was the freight of expectation. Unbeknownst to the men, this was what they came here for, every year. They were enjoying their morning, but they did not realize it. The good moments, it is true, were always this way, interstitial and unacknowledged. They craved occasion, but did not understand it. Halfway through their lives—considerably more than halfway, in several cases—the men knew nothing of their own vast contentment.

A woman entered the dining area with a boy. She paid no attention to the men in their jerseys. She briefly surveyed the continental breakfast. Then she filled two cups with orange juice, and put lids on the cups. She wrapped food in napkins, and began to arrange the food in her large purse. The boy, eight or nine, shuffled away from her, peered into the fruit bowl. He withdrew two apples and an orange. "Don't touch anything," his mother said, without looking up from the buffet. The boy turned toward the dining area, and he began to juggle the fruit. The men tapped each other on the shoulders, shifted in their chairs to watch with amusement and anxiety. They knew too well how it would end, the bruised fruit rolling beneath tables, the boy scolded once more. His face glowed with concentration. He had taught himself to juggle in his bedroom, and he was good. He would not drop the fruit. The men began to relax. They began to miss their own children. It was the best kind of missing, without pang or ache. They did not actually want to be with their children. They had fond thoughts, and were grateful for the distance that generated those thoughts. "Let's *go*, Brian," the woman said. "Right now." She zipped her bulging purse, and walked toward the lobby. As abruptly as he had begun, the boy stopped juggling. He gently caught an apple with a hand that held an apple. He wiped each piece of fruit with a napkin, placed them into the bowl, and then jogged after the woman. "We're late," the woman said. Gary, tugging at the neck of his Lawrence Taylor jersey, muttered an unkind word about the woman, and Jeff laughed. The more thoughtful among the men considered the ways in which they, too, may have become inured to the remarkable.

"JUST IMAGINE THAT," Bald Michael said. "Imagine that you're seventy-eight years old, living in Florida, reading your military history books, doing physical therapy, minding your own business. And then your daughter shows up with her new boyfriend. She's so excited for you to meet him. This guy is fifty years old. He walks with a limp. Just imagine that. It's humiliating for everyone. It's like putting a sweater on a dog."

Peter nodded, though at the mention of Florida his mind wandered to his worries about retirement income, and then to his irritation about the rapidly increasing annual dues.

The men were convened again in 324, waiting for film study. On the back of the door Carl had taped a sign-up sheet for optional afternoon haircuts, and a half dozen men clustered there with a dull pencil. Another six or seven men had gathered by the television. There was some trouble connecting the laptop to the television. What was needed, apparently, was an HDMI cable. None of the men had one, but several of the men thought simultaneously of Cyber Jim, the computer maven at Prestige Vista Solutions. According to the schedule posted outside of the conference room, Jim would be in meetings until noon.

Really, any container would have worked just fine. By holding the ends of a damp towel, Trent made a kind of sack, into which he poured all of the ping-pong balls from a green duffel bag. He shook the balls ceremoniously, and the sad and merry sound of their jostling quieted the room. Trent reached into the damp towel, and removed a ball. He squinted to ascertain Randy's name. There was no way Trent was sending Randy into that conference room. The job required some charisma. "Derek!" Trent shouted, tossing the ball quickly back into the sack.

The men clapped and cheered, chanting the name. Derek was the right guy for this. Those who were close enough to Derek reached out to touch him, slapping him on the back or punching him not forcefully on the arms. Derek was not happy to be chosen. He sat on the edge of a queen bed, jiggling his legs. Not fair, he thought.

"What's it called again?" he said.

"HDMI cable."

"And who's the guy?"

"Cyber Jim. There's a Khakis Jim, too, but it's not him."

"Careful, Derek, though, because Cyber Jim is wearing khakis."

"You really think he'll have it?" Derek said.

"Definitely."

Derek made his way through the men toward the door. The journey across the room was long and complicated.

"With your shield or on it, Derek," Gary yelled, and Steven moved in close to mitigate the historical damage.

Derek took the elevator from the third floor to the fourth floor. In Room 440 he replaced his Clint Didier jersey with a crew-neck sweater from L.L.Bean. He washed his hands and face. He stared out the window at a wet dumpster. He rode the elevator down toward the lobby. Derek thought the ball that Trent had selected from the wet towel had not looked like his ball. Of course, it was difficult to see, but Derek felt pretty sure that his ball was not as yellow as the ball Trent held aloft. Why would Trent single him out for this unpleasant task? What had he done to Trent?

Derek walked slowly through the lobby to the conference room. Here he was, looking for handouts. Hey,
brother, can you spare an A/V interface? He passed by
the conference room, but did not stop. He walked a circle
through the lobby, then another. Television, clock, fountain, pineapple, arbor. It was possible—yes, it was entirely
possible—that Derek just did not need this anymore.

The door of the conference room had a small window.
Derek peered in, but there was a presentation under way,
and the overhead lights were out. He could not see well,
and he did not, he realized, even know how to identify
Cyber Jim. His khakis, even if visible, would not very well
set him apart. A man in khakis stood at a lectern in the
front of the large room. The lectern had a reading light,
and the man was lit from beneath like a political aspirant
or an archfiend. Derek missed the hallowed space of the
conference room. Behind the man at the lectern, projected
on a screen, was a picture of a water mill. Derek could
knock, or he could simply enter. The next projected picture
was a suspension bridge. The next projected picture was a
searing desert landscape. Derek thought he heard people
laughing inside the room. The next projected picture was a
colorful hot air balloon.

"Can I help you?"

Startled, Derek turned to see a young hotel employee
in an ill-fitting uniform. A large ring of keys clipped to his
belt loop threatened to pull down his overlarge pants. He
held a brown paper bag dotted with oil spots. His left eye
twitched. Or rather, his right eye twitched. He could have

been eighteen, saving money for college, or thirty-five, with an ankle monitor. His name tag read *Robbie*.

"Sorry," Derek said. "Wrong room."

"There's only one conference room," Robbie said.

"And it's wrong," Derek said. "Sorry. Have a good day." He began walking toward the elevator.

"Are you a corporate spy?" Robbie said.

"What?"

"Should I call security?"

"There's really no need," Derek said.

Robbie laughed. "We don't have security."

"I'm moving on," Derek said. "I'm minding my own business."

"No, really," Robbie said, taking a step toward Derek. "What do you need?"

"Nothing at all."

"No, really. I'm here to help."

"There's nothing you can do," Derek said. "I was just looking for a guy who might help me get a computer cable."

"VGA?"

"No, his name is Jim."

"No—you need a VGA cable?"

"Oh. No. HDMI."

"Right," Robbie said. "Follow me."

Derek stood outside of the elevator. The bell rung, the doors slid open. He watched Robbie walk toward the front desk, his ring of keys jangling with each step. The next projected image in the conference center, which Derek could not see, was a lion bringing down a sable antelope.

The elevator doors slid closed. Derek walked toward the front desk, following Robbie against his better judgment. Robbie unlatched a swinging gate at the edge of the desk, and held it open for Derek.

Behind the front desk was an office. In the office Derek saw a desk, a chair, a bulletin board, a computer, and a large framed poster of a vibrant rose resting in two hands (cupped, Caucasian). Even in the frame, the poster was wrinkled and warped, and Derek was forced to consider that the poster concealed an escape tunnel in the wall. Robbie placed his oily paper bag on the desk, then removed his key ring from his belt loop.

"Who are you this year?" Robbie said, flipping through his keys.

"Excuse me?" Derek said.

"Which player?"

"Oh," Derek said. "This year? This year I'm L.T."

Robbie looked up from his keys, peering at Derek through his stringy bangs. Derek felt the urge to confess his lie, but he remained quiet, and Robbie resumed his search for the key.

The closet was three times larger than the office. Floor-to-ceiling shelves ran across all four walls. On the shelves were clear plastic containers of various sizes. In the containers Derek could see phones, keys, watches, dentures, hearing aids, jewelry, laptops, MP3 players, CDs, DVDs, electric toothbrushes, vibrators, gloves, mittens, dog collars, scarves, video games, GPS devices, chargers, mouthguards, neckties, shoes, shirts, pants, blouses, skirts, sweaters, knives, toys, games, headphones, hand weights, jump ropes, prescription medications, shaving kits, cosmetic bags, purses, clutches, handbags, duffel bags, garment bags, knapsacks, backpacks, satchels, wallets, hats, visors, socks, photographs, retainers, heating pads, massagers, wigs, stuffed animals, noise machines, dehumidifiers, humidifiers, sleep apnea devices, blood sugar monitors, blood pressure monitors, heart rate monitors, ear wax vacuums, dolls, Charles's brown canvas bag, sewing kits, knitting needles, thimbles, riding crops, thermometers, fingernail clippers, scissors, tweezers, books, notebooks, canes, lighters, pillows, maps, umbrellas, glasses, sunglasses, contact lens cases, porcelain figurines, travel mugs, pet food bowls, eyeshades, tennis rackets, harmonicas. In a corner there was an antique wooden crib, and wedged snugly inside the crib was Fancy Drum.

"So this is the lost and found?" Derek said.

"We just call it the lost," Robbie said, searching a low shelf. He pulled out a container full of HDMI cables, intertwined like snakes in a mating ball. "We got two-foot, four-foot, six-foot, or eight-foot," he said, pulling out cables from the container. "Whatever you want."

"I don't know," Derek said. "I guess I'll take a six-foot."

"Good choice," Robbie said. "Here, take two, just in case." He handed Derek the HDMI cables. The twitch in his eye made it difficult to tell if he had winked.

Derek nodded.

"You want anything else while we're here?" Robbie said. "You want some thumb drives?"

Derek shrugged.

Robbie scooped out a handful of thumb drives from a bottom-shelf container, and offered them to Derek.

"Thank you," Derek said, dropping the thumb drives into the front pocket of his corduroys.

Robbie looked around. "Headphones? Viagra?"

Derek moved a footstool to the corner. On the stool, on tiptoes, he reached into a container on the top shelf. Gently he pulled one end of a lavender scarf out of the container. He rubbed it between his thumb and forefinger. He read the tag to confirm it was silk.

"You like that scarf?" Robbie said.

Derek nodded.

"That's been here longer than I have," Robbie said.

"It's nice."

"You want to see other scarves? We've got boxes of scarves. I'll get them down for you."

"Don't worry about it," Derek said.

"You like that purple one."

"I like this one."

"It's all yours," Robbie said.

Derek pulled the long scarf from the container like a magician.

"Good choice," Robbie said.

"She'll love it," Robbie said.

"Hey, take it," Robbie said. "Just don't hurt me." He laughed. The keys on his belt tinkled. "Just don't snap my leg."

The ceiling light was clean and stark, as white as a ping-pong ball. The industrial dryers rumbled in the basement below. Derek folded the scarf carefully, and reached high to place it back in its container. He thanked Robbie for the cables, and set out for the lobby, wherever that might be.

THE RAIN TAPPED and streaked the windows of Room 324. With a white wand Bald Michael pulled the heavy curtains closed, darkening the room. The six-foot HDMI cable transmitted uncompressed video data from Trent's laptop to the hotel's digital television. The men settled on the beds, the chairs, the floor. They leaned forward, toward the transmitted data. They stopped talking about their parents, and grew silent. Those who chewed their nails chewed their nails. Others warmed their hands with cups of coffee. Those who had colds coughed and sneezed and sniffled and blew their noses into napkins taken from the dining area. Gary tugged at the neck of his Lawrence Taylor jersey. He plucked with agitation at the chest and shoulders. No one asked Gil to do his Frank Gifford impersonation, and he did not do it. A shower cap full of new wristbands, white and blue, was passed hand to hand across the room. Fat Michael held his helmet in his lap, absentmindedly rubbing the single bar of the face mask. His back itched in places he could not reach. There were many things George wanted to discuss, but he refrained from speaking.

Though everyone was quiet, Trent, as commissioner, called for everyone to be quiet. He placed the DVD in his laptop, and a menu materialized, whirring. Trent pressed play. The keyboard was hot to the touch. The television screen flickered for a moment, and then upon it appeared an aerial image of the Jefferson Memorial, stolid and columned, lit up from the inside at night. Far beyond the memorial there were headlights moving quickly across a dark highway, and more than one man thought to wonder who was driving those cars on that night, and what had become of them. A caption beneath the memorial read, "Live from Washington, D.C." The font was blocky and guileless, naked in its pride and enthusiasm, and it worked upon the men in ways they did not comprehend. The volume was too low, but the men could hear Frank Gifford say that it was almost Indian summer weather here in mid-November. "Turn it up," every man said, and Trent turned it up. The men could hear the bleat of the referee's whistle, indicating that the ball was ready for play.

THE MEN WOULD WATCH the play repeatedly. For over an hour the men would watch the five-second play, remembering, for a moment, as always, exactly where they were. The men would see that a play is what happens when two plays meet. The men would study this choreography of chaos and ruin. They would see, some of them, that hair on a mammoth is not progressive in any cosmic sense. Each man would see exactly where he would line up in his huddle. Steven would see, as he had seen many times before, the white towel tucked into the left side of Art Monk's waistband. He would see that Monk, lined up wide at the numbers to the left side of the formation, has his right leg forward in his stance. He would also see that Gary Clark, lined up at the numbers wide right, has his left foot forward, and he would whisper it loudly to Jeff, who would pretend not to hear him as he would see Clark disappear into the dark on a sprint route, or a seam route, or a skinny post, or a corner route. Jeff and others would be forced to assume that players who left the frame of the television camera continued to exist. Derek would see Didier doing what Didier does—that protracted series of ineffectual stutter steps against Giants linebacker Byron Hunt, whom George would see. The defensive backs would see nothing. The men would be reminded by play-by-play announcer Frank Gifford that language, always, is insufficient. "First and ten . . . Riggins . . . flea flicker . . . back to Theismann." The linemen would see the rout, the tattered pocket, blue overwhelming white. They would see the devastating pincer movement executed by Carson and Taylor. Gil would see, over and over, the majestic footwork of Redskins right tackle Mark May, who takes one step forward to sell the run, then slides back to seal the pocket and rebuff the hard outside rush of Curtis McGriff. *Every time*, over and over, knowing, as May must, that he cannot prevent the catastrophe, but doing his job simply because it's his job, pushing that rock forever. Randy, the erstwhile optician, would see that as Donnie Warren he could die for all of their sins. Tommy would see but not understand that John Riggins, whatever his virtues, is not a cunning agent of dissimulation. A mechanical actor, Riggins fails to deceive the defense, fails to divert the advance of the linebackers upon the quarterback. He turns his shoulders back to Theismann immediately upon receiving the handoff. He is not stealthy, not persuasive. It is a clumsy sleight, this Throwback Special. (As Andy remarked one year in film study—either Andy or Adam—you can't expect subtlety from a guy called the Diesel.) Nate would see that the fake run makes linebacker Harry Carson charge. Trent would see that right guard Ken Huff misses Carson as he charges. Fat Michael, the orphan, would see that the charging Carson, missed by Huff, misses Theismann, makes him step up into the pocket. Fat Michael would try to control his heart rate through deep, yogic breathing. The men would see once again that if Carson had just made the tackle, Theismann's leg would have been spared. The men would hear Frank Gifford say that Theismann is in a lot of trouble. "Theismann's in a lot of trouble," Gifford says, would say, said. Gary would see that Taylor launches himself onto Theismann's back, that he slides down Theismann's body, that his right thigh . . . Bald Michael would see that linebacker Gary Reasons jumps on Theismann after he is down, after his leg has and had been broken in two. Wesley would see that nose tackle Jim Burt jumps on Theismann after Gary Reasons jumps on Theismann. Gary (and Robert) would see that the circuit of Taylor's anguish could not be completed. Bald Michael would see that Gary Reasons prays. He would see how it is done. The men would recall that this was Theismann's 71st consecutive— and final—regular season start at quarterback. The men, excepting Steven, would not immediately recall that the Redskins won the game. The youngest of the men would recall that they were permitted to watch only the first half. The men would hear Frank Gifford say, "We'll look at it with reverse angle one more time, and I suggest, if your stomach is weak, you just don't watch." The men, many of them, would have a weak stomach, and they just wouldn't watch. A few still winced and moaned, even after all of these years. There was the year that Peter threw up a little. These men, to their great shame, had sent their wives into emergency rooms with their injured children because they could not stand the blood, the needles. The men would watch the slow-motion replay, the reverse angle replay, with their hands over their faces. The men would hear, over and over, O. J. Simpson's groaning commentary.

But first—before that—they saw the Jefferson Memorial, which George, Nate, Jeff, Adam, Wesley, Carl, Randy, and Myron had each separately visited on class field trips in elementary school. Wesley's teacher's name had actually been Mrs. Fortune. They heard Frank Gifford say that it was unseasonably warm. They read the caption "Live from Washington, D.C.," and saw that the periods were squares. The font, quaint and earnest, elicited a warm and formless memory of safety. The warm and formless memory of safety elicited by the quaint earnestness of the font made them feel mournful. The mournfulness caused by the formless memory of safety elicited by the quaint font made them feel like brimming vessels. They were alive, gloriously sad. Bald Michael had almost no hair remaining at all, just small patches above the ears, as neat as decals. The men heard the bleat of the referee's whistle, and they saw the magic circle of the huddle, inside of which the play was chanted. When the huddle broke, the offensive players, even Theismann, jogged eagerly to the line, where the defense waited. It was a home game, nationally televised. It was first and ten, near midfield, early second quarter. Everything in the playbook was available. You could run anything here. If you had a trick up your sleeve, now was a time and a down and a field position you might try it. The men watched as the players jogged to the line of scrimmage. Theismann's right leg was intact, as straight and strong as an Ionic column. Everything was early, everything was open. The things that had not happened yet were greater than the things that had happened.

THERE WAS A DEER next to the dumpster behind the hotel. It stood still in the rain, ears alert, waiting to be frightened. A grainy version of the deer occupied a small box in the third column of the fourth row of the surveillance grid of the sixteen-channel CCTV monitor at the front desk.

Like anyone shown on a surveillance monitor, the deer appeared to be involved in a crime.

In another box of the surveillance grid, the parking lot glittered blackly.

In another box, four grown men threw a football in a hallway.

In another box, two employees from the AquaDoctor scrubbed the lobby fountain with soft brushes.

In another box of the surveillance grid, the stairwell was so profoundly deserted as to seem post-human.

In another box, an elevator passenger dropped into a three-point stance.

In another box, it was very difficult to tell what exactly was going on.

In another box, a man wearing an elbow pad ran an unsustainable pace on the treadmill in the workout center.

In another box, two grown men threw a Frisbee in a hallway.

In another box, the continental breakfast had long since ended.

In another box, was that a cat in a hallway?

In another box, inhabitants of the conference center applauded silently.

In another box of the surveillance monitor, the front desk clerk ignored the sixteen-channel surveillance monitor.

In another box, a man pacing and gesticulating alone in a hallway was either suffering from mental illness or using a phone with a hands-free headset.

In another box, an upside-down bird gnawed grainily on the knotted rope in its cage.

In the final box, an elderly man walked with purpose and a dignified limp through the lobby doors, into the hotel, vanishing from the box. He then reappeared in the front desk box, placing his elbows on the desk in a manner that seemed both inquisitive and assertive. He spoke with the front desk clerk—he appeared to speak with the front desk clerk—then walked briskly out of the box. The elderly man reappeared in the elevator box, pressing buttons, or more likely pressing a single button repeatedly. Here, in the elevator, you could see him well. He was perhaps seventy-five, with a full head of neatly trimmed gray hair. He was tall, with excellent posture. He wore a plaid shirt tucked into dark pants, but it was not difficult to imagine him wearing a uniform of some sort. The man did not, like almost all passengers, look at himself in the mirror on the back wall of the elevator. After a time, the elevator doors opened, and he exited the box. He reappeared in a different box of the sixteen-box surveillance grid, walking toward a group of grainy men throwing a football in a hallway. Most of the men dispersed immediately, though one of the men stood against the wall as if frozen. His face, which was not clearly visible on the surveillance monitor, had a startled expression. The abandoned football still spun on the hallway carpet like the altimeter dial of a rapidly descending aircraft. Midway down the hall, the elderly man stopped outside of a room, and knocked on the door. The vending alcove was neither visible nor audible. The man appeared to say something to the door. One is forced to assume that he was viewed through the peephole. Eventually, the door opened, and the elderly man entered the room, disappearing from the box in the fourth column of the second row of the surveillance grid. By this time the deer, too, was gone from the box with the deer in it.

IN THE LOBBY, Wesley walked circles around the fountain, where a quality control representative on break from the Prestige Vista Solutions retreat was talking to the workers from the AquaDoctor about ornamental carp. Wesley's daughter was having trouble sleeping because someone at school had told her that Jesus got pinned to the arch for his belief system, but right now Wesley needed to concentrate on Giants nose tackle Jim Burt. What Wesley needed to keep in mind, according to Steven, was that Burt was undrafted out of the University of Miami. As Burt, Wesley had the not-insignificant role of pushing hard up the middle, then diving belatedly onto a screaming pile containing Theismann. The key was to wait for Gary Reasons, played by Bald Michael, to dive late onto Theismann, whose leg was already fractured by Taylor, before he commenced his own late dive onto Theismann's fractured leg. There were two late hits—Reasons had the early late hit, and Burt had the late late hit. Burt had invented the Gatorade shower, Steven said. The rhythmic whisper of the soft brushes against the tiles of the fountain sounded like a mother putting her baby to sleep. Wesley, at any rate, had to remain patient. He had to have an internal clock, Steven said. He had to make certain he did not get too excited and dive prematurely late, as certain Burts had in previous years. (Gary's Burt, four or five years ago, arrived at Theismann almost before Taylor.) Wesley's uniform had pizza sauce on the shoulder stripes. "Do you mean nailed to the cross?" Wesley had said to his daughter, immediately regretting it. He had chosen to care about accuracy, correctness. Why? The child had seemed fragile ever since the squirrels had mutilated her jack-o'-lantern. "Hey, look, it just makes it spookier," Wesley had said, holding up the mauled pumpkin, but the child was inconsolable. Her worry box was full. "This is not something that just started," Wesley's wife had said. "She's always been like this." "She's just overly sensitive," Wesley said. "That's exactly what I'm talking about," his wife had said. Wesley missed his children, the gay son in college, the troubled girl at home. He wanted them not to suffer, even though he knew suffering was important. He wanted them not to have more than their fair share. He was helping to raise sensitive children. That was the worst kind of children, the most painful. "He came back to life, though, honey," Wesley had said of Jesus, immediately regretting it. It was the early afternoon, Saturday, but as he walked around the fountain Wesley imagined his daughter sleeping. That was the time he loved her best. That was the only time she wasn't running her mouth. That was the only time she wasn't explaining the world, trying to make it safe with her words. The workers from the AquaDoctor and the quality control representative from Prestige Vista Solutions looked up to see the elderly man walking through the lobby, lightly gripping the arm of a nondescript Caucasian male, perhaps forty-five, with brown hair (streaked gray), receding hairline, pale and puffy and carelessly shaven face, rogue hair growth in ears and nostrils, bushy eyebrows, yellowed teeth, vitamin deficiency, wrinkles around eyes, some dark spots on face and hands, maybe six-feet-two in college but now shorter, about one ninety or one ninety-five with an incipient gut, a slight limp, no visible scars or tattoos, a slightly enlarged prostate, wearing ill-fitting jeans, a pilly sweater from Target, and a light jacket with a dry sheen. The two men were clearly father and son—you could see it in their walk—but the elderly man had aged far better than the younger man. The father's grip on the son's arm was less about support than custody. The younger man carried a duffel bag.

The front desk clerk looked down from the father and son to watch the father and son grainily traverse a small box on the sixteen-channel surveillance monitor. "We could carve the other side of the pumpkin," Wesley had said to his daughter. "We could get another pumpkin," he had said. "We could go eat the squirrels' food," he had said, pretending to dig up nuts with his paws. "Honey," he had said to his daughter, "those Bible stories were translated." Wesley, circling the fountain, preparing intently for his role as nose tackle Jim Burt, did not see Adam's father leading Adam out of the hotel.

•

CARL WASN'T a particularly gifted barber, but he had all of the equipment—the cape, the dull scissors, the electric clippers with a cord that was too short. He had cut hair in college to make money, and for a dozen or so years now he had offered cuts to the men on the afternoon of the Throwback Special. The haircuts were optional, free, and private. Carl's clippers glistened with golden oil. The men signed up for fifteen-minute appointments, but they all tended to arrive at Carl's room at the time of the first appointment. The man with the first appointment went in alone, while the others waited in a line in the hallway, seated against the wall in the order of appointment. Some men in the hall had no appointment, and just came for the company. Thus, the ritual was communal, but only in the hallway, where the men laughed and talked, while the clippers buzzed faintly behind the door. Carl had nothing to do with this arrangement. He would have welcomed all of the men in the room together. He would in fact have preferred chatter and merriment and derision to solemnity and isolation, which he found exhausting. But the custom reflected the will of the men, for whom the haircut was as private as a urological exam. The custom arose spontaneously, and it was perpetuated without consideration. A haircut by an acquaintance required submission, and submission required privacy. The man sat, he wore a musty cape, heavy as a welcome mat. Carl sprayed his hair with a water bottle and combed it, humiliatingly, straight

183

forward. There was no mirror. Drops of water ran down the man's nose. His face itched, but he did not scratch it. His arms were trapped beneath the heavy cape. He was a child again, a boy. His thoughts drifted toward his mother. The standing barber circled his chair, carelessly bumped him, wiped water from his face, hair from his ears. The barber leaned down close, breathing heavily, smelling like a man. His forearms were hairy. The barber talked, or he didn't. The barber cut the hair however he wanted to cut it, regardless of request or instruction. He moved the man's head up, down. The barber nicked him—the neck, the tips of the ears—then dabbed the blood roughly with a towel. The man resented this optional experience that he craved. When a man came out of Carl's room, the other men whistled and made loud noises at him. They made fun of his haircut, made fun of Carl. "What did he *do* to you?" Then it would grow quiet in the hallway, and the next man would stand and knock gravely on the locked door.

3:00: *Peter*

Peter's hair was wavy and wiry. It was brittle and lifeless, like something partially buried in an ancient seabed. It was both thick and thinning. At the crown of his head a turbulent cowlick seemed to be churning toward landfall, forcing evacuation in low-lying areas. Carl had never given Peter the same cut twice, and the sight of the swirling cowlick made him nervous and angry. To cut hair was to love order, but Peter's scalp was the site of radical turmoil. Not even a skilled barber could have done much with it. The hair, though, was only part of the issue. Peter was, as the ancient barbers whom Carl had worked with in college would have said, a *leaker*. Some people, almost as soon as you lay that heavy cape across their shoulders and put your hands to their heads, begin to lose the solid self. Peter removed his mouthguard, the emotional levee. He was trying to tell Carl about the children's choir's fall concert, and he could not finish. The sound from those rented risers . . . Carl was annoyed, but he knew what to do. He had watched the old-timers. He tucked the scissors into his back pocket, and he picked up the spray bottle from the bedside table. He did not move quickly, but neither did he move slowly. With the spray bottle, he sprayed water onto Peter's head. He sprayed and sprayed, combing forward. He doused Peter's head until streams of water ran down Peter's face. Peter knew to keep his hands beneath the cape. Carl sprayed. It was an old trick, a ruthless courtesy.

3:15:   *Gil*

When Peter emerged into the hallway, Gil obligatorily made fun of his haircut, then knocked on the door of Carl's room. Carl opened the door, and nodded hello. Gil sat down in the chair, located between the two beds. Beneath the chair Carl had spread out four white hotel towels. Both men were mildly embarrassed by the sudden realization that they would face each other that evening in a battle of strength and agility, albeit a ceremonial one with assumed identities and a predetermined outcome. Carl placed the heavy cape on Gil. They both looked straight forward, as if into a mirror. The heating and cooling unit ticked and clanked. Carl winced as he absentmindedly prodded the tender lump with the comb. He gave Gil an opportunity to say what he wanted, but Gil said nothing, so Carl tilted Gil's head down and began to cut the hair on the back of his head with clippers. The cord of the clippers was a taut line, but it did not pull out of the wall socket. Gil closed his eyes, as if in prayer. The vibration of the clippers felt nice along his cranium. He could hear the men in the hallway, laughing and shouting, passing the long afternoon. Two voices rose above the others. To Gil it sounded as if George and Steven were hashing something out, though he could not discern the subject, nor did he wish to. Their tone and cadence—adversarial, intimate—carried much more meaning than their words, which were probably inane. The loud discussion through a wall, combined perhaps with the weather, made him sleepy and nostalgic. Gil had a long drive the next day. He loved his family, but he didn't want to go home. He was having fun—though *fun* may not have been the right word. He was happy here—though *happy* may not have been the right word.

3:30: *Nate*

"Is it true about Adam?" Nate asked.

A barber, even one isolated in a hotel room, was expected to know things.

"I don't know," Carl said.

From his wallet Nate produced a photograph of his children, posed in an artificial bower. The girl was skinny, with dark circles beneath her eyes, and she clung like a castaway to the gleaming trunk of a synthetic tree.

"Nice," Carl said.

"Turns out she was allergic to that plastic bark," Nate said. "She's allergic to everything, though. When we were kids, Carl—do you remember?—there was one, maybe two allergies."

"Bees," Carl said, trimming the hair above Nate's ear.

"That's right," Nate said. He seemed to be making a moral argument. "There was that kid who bragged that he would die if he got stung. Then there was pollen, and maybe cats. And that was it. That was all. And now I've got a kid who is allergic to crayons and dust."

Carl stood and moved behind Nate's chair. He nodded, though there was no mirror.

"Aren't we supposed to become better adapted through generations?" Nate said. He sounded troubled. He seemed to be suggesting that children today did not share our values.

Out in the hallway, something or someone slammed hard against the door, and the men laughed and coughed. Then Nate told a story. The story began with a kind of rustling or scuttling sound in the basement. Carl gritted his teeth. God help me, he thought, this is going to be a story about an animal in the house. Carl had been at the hotel for a little more than twenty-four hours, and he had already heard six or seven stories about animals in houses, identical in dramatic contour—the strange noise or scat or smell, the mystery, the false hypothesis, the persistence, the breakthrough, the discovery, the grim and triumphant resolution. The unstated moral: *It's my house.* But Carl tried to be patient, he did. He understood that each animal in each house felt unique to the home owner. A man with an animal in his house is an archetype. He joins a long narrative tradition, and yet for each particular man in each particular house the event is not allegory. It is an urgent and singular encounter, exceptional and unrepeatable. Carl remembered very clearly the bats in his own attic. Those terrible little fingers. He knew that each man was entitled to his story about an animal in the house, and he tried to pay attention, tried to nod and sound surprised when it turned out to be a raccoon. "Are you serious?" Carl said. "What did you do then?" Nate had good hair, and it was a pleasure to cut. He had, at least in the decade that Carl had known him, always parted his hair in the middle. It was time, Carl thought, for a change.

3:45: _Adam_

(Carl was worried that he was dying, though he was not. He stood in his room by the door. He could hear the men in the hallway—it must be nearly all of them, maybe more—but nobody knocked. He placed his clippers on top of the television. His hands were covered with graying hair and streaks of black marker. He walked to the window, and looked out at the parking lot. The sky had descended, and seemed now to rest upon the hotel, raining upon it. The day was growing dark, and Carl pulled the curtains together. The sign-up sheet was posted on the outside of the room's door, and Carl did not know which men were waiting in line, or how many. He did not necessarily enjoy cutting hair anymore, if he ever did, but he continued out of a sense of obligation. He put three pills on his tongue, sprayed water into his mouth from the spray bottle. He lay on his bed and closed his eyes. He should not have attended his high school reunion last month. That had been a mistake. The best-case scenario was that Carl was halfway through his life. It was alternately a comfort and a terror to consider that you were halfway through your life, but at any rate it was not an accurate concept. You were never actually halfway through your life. Not really. Not in the sense that you were halfway though a cord of winter firewood, or a tank of gas, or a trip home from the beach, or the one cocktail you allowed yourself on a weeknight. Halfway through something, that is, whose wholeness is a given, preexistent. You were always, instant by instant, at the very edge of your life, at the end of it, in its entirety, and so never at any point, Carl considered, in the middle. Adam did not show up. Perhaps the rumor was true. It would certainly not be the first time that a man had been retrieved, though this time felt more grave, Carl thought. He imagined an automotive fleet in tight highway forma-tion, steadily approaching the hotel. A wave of relations, each determined to find a man and bring him home.)

4:00: _Randy_

Randy sat in the chair between the beds. The chair was now encircled by a thick ring of cut hair. He felt as if he were in a nest. Carl sprayed Randy's hair, and combed it straight forward. Water dripped from Randy's nose. Carl leaned down in front of Randy to cut the bangs across Randy's forehead. Randy confessed, as Carl knew he would. He told Carl the truth about the Jeff Bostic uniform. "It's true that I sold it," he said, telling the story from the beginning, or well before it. And in the six minutes he had remaining in his appointment, he had other things to tell Carl, as well. In forty-six years Randy had done any number of things of which he was ashamed. There was nothing interesting, nothing unusual. Carl had heard it all many times. Randy had lied, he had stolen, he had cheated, he had hurt people who loved him. He had once peed in a bottle of Mellow Yellow, knowing full well his older sister would ask him for a drink . . . If he wanted, Randy, like everyone else, could tell his life story as an outright spree of wickedness and deceit.

4:15: _Dennis_

Dennis was a business traveler, staying alone on the second floor. He sat quietly for his trim. Out in the hallway, the men had dispersed, leaving behind some trash and a notable silence. Carl concentrated on the hair of Dennis, and he cut well, though it depleted him. Dennis's cough drop gradually filled the room with its scent of medicine and childhood. The smell had not changed in decades. It must be the case that people did not actually want cough drops to taste like cherry, like lemon. In the absence of much ambient noise, the smell of the cough drop began nearly to drone. Suddenly, Dennis said something. He asked Carl if he would mind trimming his eyebrows. Carl could think of no reason to refuse, and he trimmed the eyebrows, holding his breath to steady his hands. When the appointment was over, Carl wiped Dennis's neck and ears with a towel. He carefully removed the cape. "There you go," he said, as barbers do. Dennis nodded, stood. For some time he stared at a watercolor of horses in a pasture, as if at a mirror. Carl sat on the bed. Dennis reached for his wallet, and Carl braced himself for more photographs of children. It was more than he could handle. Dennis removed fourteen dollars from his wallet, and placed the bills on the bedside table.

4:30:   _Michael_

Fat Michael entered the room as Dennis left. He saw Carl sitting on the bed, shoulder against the headboard, eyes closed, mouth open, scissors dangling from his finger. He was either asleep or pretending to be asleep, and there was no real difference that Fat Michael could determine. The amount of cut hair on the floor was disconcerting, unseemly. The room was a scene of unpleasant fecundity, as one might discover beneath a rock or a rotting log. Fat Michael thought it distasteful that the men should have left so much of themselves here, as if they had molted. Slowly, Carl's shoulder slid down the headboard. He lay on the bed on his back with his feet still on the floor. The scissors dropped to the carpet. Fat Michael's hair really wasn't that long, anyway. He didn't need a cut, and he didn't think much of Carl's skills as a barber. He had just signed up to fill out the schedule, so that Carl wouldn't feel bad. He picked up Carl's scissors from the floor. They did not seem like good scissors. The blades rattled loosely, and small spots of rust dotted the handles. Fat Michael considered that the men should pitch in to buy Carl a new pair, or perhaps a whole new barber's kit. When was Carl's birthday? He glanced around for Carl's wallet, but did not see it. Fat Michael's birthday was today, but nobody knew it. He had never mentioned it, and he couldn't very well mention it now, after so many years. He put the scissors on the chair, and left the room quietly. He knew the men would never buy Carl a new barber's kit. It was enough to imagine the generosity.

THE YEAR Jeff brought his girlfriend; the year nobody brought a football; the year Trent slept in the lobby; the flu year; the food poisoning year; the year the conference room had just been painted; the year that George was Theismann; the year that George was commissioner; the year that George was Taylor; 2001; the year Myron forgot to make room reservations; the year Vince shocked himself with the toaster; the year the linebackers got stuck on the roof; the very first year; the year the smokers found that big box of fireworks by the dumpster; the year Wesley dropped his watch in the fountain; the year Steven got so drunk and stole a ladder; the year that Tommy disappeared for a good long while; the year of the flight attendants; the year that Adam called Gil in the middle of the night, pretending to be the real Theismann; the snow year; the lightning year; the year Charles lost his shit; the year Fat Michael lost his wedding ring; the year Randy broke his wrist; the year Nate dislocated his elbow; the year of Bald Michael's toupee; the year Fancy Drum was vandalized; the year Derek's car was vandalized; the years that guy Danny had to fill in as a substitute, and kept trying to sell the rest of the men those specialty candles; the year the newspaper reporter was supposed to come; the year the cops came and arrested the night desk clerk; the year of the hot wings contest; the year that Robert was not the first to arrive; the year Carl fumbled the snap; the year the hotel ran out of breakfast; the year the hotel ran out of hot water; the year Nate's wife went into labor; the year of babies; the year Gary made his big announcement; the year of the carbon dioxide dragsters.

Myron, Gil, and Tommy sat on a couch in the lobby, waiting for others to come down for dinner. All three had heard birds flying smack into their glass patio doors. All three were just praying their kids would get scholarships. The fountain was half full, and gurgling unhealthily.

Jerry, the transportation director for Prestige Vista Solutions, walked past the men on the couch and wished them good luck this evening. The men nodded, thanked Jerry.

"Big night," Jerry said.

The men concurred. Myron had a startled expression on his face.

"Last year, right?" Jerry said.

Gil took off his reading glasses, and cleaned them with his shirt. The elevator bell rang twice. Tommy stared down at his hands, folded in his lap. Myron said, "What?"

"This is the last year, right?" Jerry said.

"Who told you that?" Gil said.

"A guy yesterday," Jerry said. "I don't know his name. Guy with a chinstrap. Was it some kind of secret?"

The men shook their heads. "No," Myron said. "Of course not."

"Take it easy," Jerry said, walking toward the automatic doors of the lobby. "Have fun."

The fountain gurgled. The desk clerk read *Dune*. The bright, enormous clock bathed the entire lobby in time. Each of the three men on the couch assumed that the other two men had known, that he was the only one who had not. Each felt the sting of exclusion, the ancient wound, before anger rushed in like an antibody. Why had he not been told? Why had he been treated like a child?

They sat in silence, staring up at the television, the muted anchors. Each man was indignant. Beneath the indignation there was an exotic and diverse world of feeling, as dark as an ocean trench.

BY CUSTOM the men ate dinner with positional mates. By custom they made their way in clusters down the dirt path along the service road, ducking under the heavy wet branches of evergreens. By custom they ate inexpensive food with sauce packets. By custom they ate in silence. There was, after all, no reason to say that Theismann's right leg remains to this day shorter than his left, or that the sound by his own account was like two muzzled gunshots or that the surgeons at Arlington Hospital had to wash the wound dozens of times with saline solution in an attempt to prevent infection. ("You start with a gallon," one of the surgeons said, and the men did not.) There was no need to say that Theismann described the injury as a kind of death, followed by rebirth. Straws squeaked inside the lids of fountain drinks. Boys within the plastic tunnels of the restaurant's Play Zone taunted other boys, and then injured themselves attempting to flee. By tradition the man playing Theismann and the man playing Taylor stayed away from each other, like a bride and groom before a wedding. Nobody ate all that much.

Back in their rooms, the men helped each other pull

Chris Bachelder

jerseys over shoulder pads. They helped each other tape fingers and wrists, tie shoelaces. By tradition, each man would drive to Warren G. Harding Middle School alone. Nobody would carpool. They left the hotel in full uniform, carrying their wallets and keys inside their helmets. That sound, vaguely martial, was their cleats across the parking lot.

- 6 -
THE PLAY

"**W**AIT, DO YOU EVEN KNOW WHERE IT IS?"
"It's supposed to be over here."
"Is it a stadium?"
"No, it's a field at a middle school. We're close."
"A football field?"
"Yes."
"Middle schools have football fields?"
"What are you talking about?"
"Why would a middle school need a football field?"
"Where are you from?"
"New Hampshire."
"There are lights over there."
"Where?"
"See the lights?"

Brandon turned left at a stoplight, and drove his Toyota through the wet streets toward the distant yellow glow of a light tower. Sarah sat in the passenger seat beside Brandon, smoothing the suitcase folds out of her jeans. Paul and Deirdre sat in the back with not enough leg room. They were all young sale associates for Prestige Vista Solutions, two or three years out of college. After a day in the conference room, they felt like falsely convicted inmates exonerated by DNA evidence. The interior of the sedan was humid with fertility and body spray. The seat belts seemed like a form of sexual restraint, a precaution. Deirdre put her cheek against the cold glass of the window. At a stoplight a man in an expensive car smiled at her, and waved. She did not smile back or wave, but she received his attention, and kept it.

All of the young sale associates agreed, riding through the night, that the new commissions program would be excellent if they got a lot of sales, less desirable if they did not. They all privately liked Kevin, the team leader, but they laughed about the sweat stains, the pants, the screen-saver of the ugly baby and the dog.

"There's the parking lot," Paul said.

"Do we need tickets or anything?" Sarah said.

"I doubt it."

Only the women had umbrellas. They offered to share them, but the men declined. Sarah found a ring of wet keys on the ground next to a car, and she rested them on the handle of the driver's-side door. Paul cradled a backpack beneath the front of his jacket as they walked toward the field, where football players stretched and jogged and performed jumping jacks beneath rain and low wisps of fog. The grass was patchy and brown, dotted with dark puddles. It was not lined with chalk. A distant goalpost lay on its side in the mud, mired like a mastodon in a tar pit. Two leaning light towers draped a feeble glow onto the field, accentuating the vast darkness beyond. At the far end of the field a scoreboard with missing lights showed seven points for the home team and seven for the visitor, with an indecipherable number of minutes remaining in what appeared to be the second quarter. Above the scoreboard a wooden sign welcomed fans to the Falcons Nest, and beneath it stood a man in a yellow poncho. In the cold rain, alone beneath a dilapidated scoreboard and a grammatical error, the man had the posture of one who was enduring a severe test of faith from a higher power.

Several long wooden benches ran crookedly along one sideline. On the other sideline there was a narrow block of aluminum bleachers, which wobbled and creaked as the young sales associates climbed to the top row. "Luxury box," Brandon said. Sarah had thought to bring two hotel towels, and she wiped the bench dry. The four sat close together beneath the two feminine umbrellas, their pockets buzzing intermittently with text messages from their boyfriends and girlfriends back home. They were all conscious of attempting to have a memorable night, and of having one.

"When are you due?" Deirdre asked Paul, pointing at the backpack tucked beneath the front of his jacket.

"Any day now," Paul said, rubbing his belly.

"*Push*," Deirdre said.

Paul extricated the backpack, and unzipped it. He liked having something to do, and he liked the way Deirdre's upper arm, beneath her jacket and sweater, felt against his upper arm, beneath his jacket and sweater. "I am the proud mother," he said, "of a party." He removed from the backpack four plastic cups and a bottle of sparkling wine that could be, if necessary, a joke. A nice bottle of champagne would have made it look like he was trying too hard, but in fact he had tried very hard to make it look as if he was not trying too hard. It had taken him almost half an hour to find a bottle of sparkling wine that seemed versatile enough to pass for either thoughtful or parodic, and perhaps both. He wanted to let the night decide. Now he draped a folded wet towel over his arm. He was suddenly a maître d', not a new mother. Deirdre laughed, as did Paul and Sarah. He put the towel over the bottle, and expertly removed the cork from the inexpensive sparkling wine. The happy, expensive sound of it. When he poured, he tilted the cups at forty-five-degree angles to minimize the loss of bubbles. He had worked for a catering company in college. As he poured, he glanced at Sarah's face, trying to determine the meaning of his own gift. Drops of rain slid from the edge of the umbrella into the cups of sparkling wine. Paul wanted to say something in French, but he had forgotten all of it. There was also in the backpack a box of cookies, a festive assortment. The women each selected a cookie, and the men took three. They clicked plastic cups, drank to the core values of Prestige Vista Solutions.

"So which one is David?"

"He's . . . right there. Number twenty-three."

"Blue or white?"

"Blue."

"I don't see him."

"He's right over there. Williams."

"That's not his last name, is it?"

"No. He's playing someone else."

"I see him."

"He's basically the only one out there who looks like he ought to be wearing that uniform."

"Except that guy. Seven."

"How did he get into this?"

"He said he was approached in the lobby. He basically had to interview for it. They were short a man."

"Do they play a whole game?"

"Who knows?"

"Are you boys disappointed you didn't get chosen?"

Paul and Brandon laughed at the absurd question. They were in fact disappointed, but they didn't know it. Their wistful envy, by the time it made its way to their minds, had been transmuted to mild disdain and nonchalance and embarrassment. Paul said he had been in the elevator with some of the men, and they were ridiculous. Brandon agreed. He had seen them at breakfast. Just shoot him, Brandon said, if he's doing that when he gets to be their age.

"Oh, they're not so bad," Sarah said.

Now there were two other spectators, a hooded man sitting in the first row of the bleachers, and another man in a baseball cap in the third row. They both sat hunched, still and watchful, arms crossed for warmth. The man in the baseball cap unclasped himself to pour a drink from a dented thermos. The men on the field progressed slowly through orchestrated series of movements, like tai chi masters in the park.

"There's just some people who shouldn't wear football pants," Brandon said.

"These guys are going to get *hurt*," Paul said, and the man in the baseball cap turned his head briefly.

Someone on the field whistled. The football was placed on the ground in a patch of limp grass, then each team gathered in a huddle. The Giants huddle was rapidly generated and ill-formed. It dissolved almost immediately, and the defenders spread out in rough formation, awaiting the offensive alignment. The Redskins huddle was a perfect and intimate order, elemental and domestic, like a log cabin in the wilderness. Sarah and Deirdre, Brandon and Paul—they could perhaps sense in the huddle the origins of civilization. The men bent at the waist, hands on knees. Their helmets nearly touched inside the private sphere, where ten men listened for the secret, the invocation against evil. Their breath rose together from the center of the circle. They broke their huddle with a synchronized and disciplined clap, not bright but dulled by gloves and tape. They jogged to the line of scrimmage. Even the quarterback jogged. He wore number 7. His face mask was old-fashioned, a single bar. It was nearly ten o'clock, November 18. The rain fell steadily through the fog. Passing cars honked from the street, and a passenger in a truck yelled something mean-spirited and vulgar. It was odd, Paul thought, not to begin with a kickoff. He did not know what he hoped to see, failure or something else. The quarterback was under center. He looked to his right and then to his left. He looked again to his right, then to his left. He called, "Yellow forty-one," his voice wavering. He called it again. The hooded man and the man with the baseball cap leaned forward, elbows on their knees. The sales associates sat closely together on the top row of the bleachers, their shoulders touching. The man in the yellow poncho stood completely still beneath the scoreboard. The ball was snapped then, and something happened, a single ruinous play, a discrete unit of chaos, violent and unlovely. The players grunted, their damp pads clacked through the fog. The entire play lasted perhaps five seconds. "Shit, flea flicker," Brandon murmured as the running back pitched the ball back to the quarterback. "Uh-oh," he said. "Throw it, *throw* it." But the quarterback had not thrown the ball. He had stepped up into the pocket to avoid the rush, and then crumpled beneath a linebacker who had leaped onto his back. "That was not good," Paul said. "Those old guys are not up for this." Other defenders jumped on top of the quarterback, and a muffled scream came from the pile of bodies. Like a spell the scream lifted the players from the pile. One player, the one who had brought the quarterback down, gestured frantically to an empty sideline. He put his hands on his helmet. It was something the sales associates would remember.

Sarah stood up, nearly spilling her wine from the plastic cup. "What is he doing?" she said. "What was that? What happened? Is someone hurt?" The other associates shrugged and shook their heads. The hooded man in the first row of the bleachers was standing, applauding. The sound of his solitary appreciation was small in the night. Paul checked once more to see if the bottle was empty. Perhaps, he thought, it would be best to just go to bed early. Tomorrow was another long day of meetings. "Was that real?" Sarah said. "Is it over? Are they leaving?"

ROOM 324 WAS WARM and pungent, suffused with the smell of leaf rot and liniment. The muddy cleats teemed in a pile by the door. The men embraced, they tousled hair, they pounded one another on the shoulder pads. They drank inexpensive sparkling wine from the bottle, chewed unlit cigars, passed ice packs and Carl's dull scissors. Their cheeks and knuckles were red from the cold, and their fingers were stiff. As was increasingly the case in recent years, several men were injured. They had pulled something, tweaked something, strained something. They grimaced, gripped the tender regions. They cut tape from their ankles and wrists, and it lay on the carpet in withered, valedictory strips. It was clear to everyone that this had been their best Throwback Special. Steven was challenged to deny it, and he would not. He said he just wanted to check his notes, but he could not check them because Bald Michael had hidden his notes in the second-floor vending alcove.

Tommy's eyes shone wild with frantic relief. Because he had been so nervous, because he had been so concerned about handling the football, because he was not particularly dexterous or graceful, he had been the perfect Riggins, the standard. He had turned his shoulders too quickly, pitched it back too quickly. He had been utterly unconvincing in performing the flea flicker, which is to say he had been utterly convincing in performing Riggins. The best Riggins—Tommy had made this evident to all—was a bad Riggins. And Tommy, like other men, had somehow actualized himself while pretending to be someone else. He snuck up behind Myron with a finger to his lips. He clasped his arms around Myron's stomach, and lifted him off the floor. Myron kicked Gil's drink out of his hand, and he spilled his own drink on the comforter. Someone blotted halfheartedly with a sock. Tommy's mustache, other men began to realize, was gone. He had, at some unknown point, removed it.

Randy held his hand in a bucket of ice. His Donnie Warren had been all truth. He had been elegantly wrecked by Taylor, and he wore the dark mud stain across his chest. He had even gotten his hand stepped on while lying on the ground, a nice touch. The hand, now submerged in a bucket of ice, looked both swollen and bony. Vince took a picture of Randy's hand in the bucket, pink and blurry beneath the cubes like a creature whose existence has been rumored but not verified. Vince put his hand on Randy's shoulder, and Randy allowed it, leaned into it. He got glimpses now and then. He sensed that the loss of his eyewear business might be a blessing. That was what people tended to say about the very worst things. That was the outrageous claim they made. In his garage where he did not kill himself he had constructed a prototype of a self-washing house window. He had used a voltaic cell to power the wiper, but his design called for solar. His hand might have been broken. It throbbed beneath the ice in a nearly pleasurable way.

Gil sat on a queen bed with the other offensive linemen. He had removed his shoulder pads, but he still wore with pride the jersey of Mark May. Despite the rain and the mud, his jersey was immaculate, shimmering. The offensive line had worked perfectly as a unit. Each man had done his job. Others paid passing tribute with oinks and snorts, cans of beer. Gil leaned back on the bed, striking something hard beneath the comforter, a large cylindrical lump. He flung back the blanket and sheets, and there was Fancy Drum. The linemen cheered. Across the room, Steven tried to pretend that it did not matter much to him one way or the other. Men who had detested Fancy Drum now looked upon it with affection, tenderness. The drum seemed to have proven itself, completed a rite of passage. It was now, at last, at the end, accepted into the group. Men posed for photos, not one of them lewd, an arm around Fancy Drum, as around a teenage nephew.

George put in a terrible CD of his brother's jam band, and Wesley replaced it immediately. Without removing his helmet, Fat Michael poured corn chips from a bag into his mouth. He swigged sparkling wine through the single crossbar of the face mask, and he danced to the music, without inhibition or rhythm. He seemed reluctant to put any weight on his right leg. His jersey was a mess. Jeff stayed close by, keeping an eye on Fat Michael. It was almost always the case that the man who played Theismann had to be monitored for a few hours after the play.

David, the young Web specialist at Prestige Vista Solutions, parted the curtains to watch the rain. He had the odd sensation that he might see the players, himself included, beneath the foggy dim lights of the distant field. He closed the curtains, and attempted to cross the room, his backpack slung over one shoulder pad. Along the way, he was heartily thanked and congratulated. His hair was tousled, his back was slapped, his hand was shaken. He was given a red plastic cup, and another. Waiting outside the bathroom, David asked Vince what he should do with his uniform, his gear. Vince shrugged. "Souvenir," he said. "A small token. Or give it to Trent." He shrugged again, and gestured to David that the bathroom was now unoccupied.

In the bathroom, trying with cold fingers to untie the drawstring of his pants, David decided that he would not, after all, blog about the night, or post any pictures. He didn't have any pictures. He resisted looking at himself in the mirror, perhaps out of a concern that his bright reflection would almost certainly tell the wrong story. He liked wearing the uniform, though it was faded and frayed. He had liked the snug fit of the helmet, the reassuring pressure of the chinstrap. He had liked the stillness before the snap, his breath in the air. He had liked the sense that anything at all might happen, even though only one thing could happen. And he had liked watching the old grainy replay on his tablet. The antique font, the primitive production values. It was like watching newsreel footage of some distant war or assassination attempt. With his back to the mirror David took off his uniform and pads, while the men outside the bathroom sang the hit song from a recent animated movie about Pegasus. He folded the jersey and pants, and placed them on the edge of the bathtub. He put the helmet and shoulder pads in the tub, and did not take a picture of them. His regular clothes, drab and wrinkled, were stuffed in his backpack. He began slowly to dress.

Back by the window, next to the heating and cooling unit, Charles told Robert that it did not sound serious. He wore his brown canvas bag over his uniform, the strap running diagonally across his Terry Kinard jersey. He put his hand on Robert's arm. "It sounds to me," he said, "like she's just a picky eater. I wouldn't worry too much. But get in touch with me if you have any more concerns or questions." He reached into his bag for a business card. Robert tucked the card into his maroon waistband, next to his ping-pong ball, and walked directly into the throng, forlorn and euphoric. The men did not think of Adam, whose departure had been so mysterious, so generic.

The door opened. Chad entered with more ice, and the cat darted from the room. The phone rang on the bedside table, but nobody answered it. Peter held a deck of cards, and several men implored him to do the trick he had done the previous year, or was it two years ago? The trick was called "Three Ladies and a Rascal." Derek finally found Gary, who had taken off his Lawrence Taylor jersey and draped it over the television. Derek wanted to know what it was like. He was curious, not angry. The room was so loud that the men had to lean close to speak and hear.

Gary shrugged. "It was a weight," he said.

Derek leaned toward Gary's ear. "A wait?"

Gary nodded. "A big weight."

Trent stood in the narrow alley between the wall and the bed. He surveyed the room, nodding. He was satisfied with his work as commissioner. He had had to make some difficult decisions. He had had to guide the group through some unprecedented challenges. He had had to clean a nasty bloodstain out of a jersey in the middle of the night. He reached across the bed to shake hands with Vince, Bald Michael, Gil, Wesley.

"Time to write your memoirs," Gil said to Trent.

Typically, the commissioner's final duty as commissioner was to select the next commissioner, but Trent could see that the ping-pong balls had at some point been dumped on a bed, and were now dispersed entropically throughout the room—beneath furniture, under the curtain, in the cleat pile. One ball was in the bathroom. Two had been stepped on and dented. One was held tightly in Randy's noninjured hand. One was stuck to a curled piece of athletic tape like a mouse in a trap. It was not a process, Trent observed, that could be easily reversed.

"Guys," he said.

"Hey, guys," he said.

Carl stood on a queen bed. His jersey was untucked, and his thigh pads and knee pads had shifted radically away from his thighs and knees. He turned in a circle. He could see everything from up this high. He tried to kick a ping-pong ball, and missed. Andy shuffled past the bed with a bottle of sparkling wine. "Trick or treat!" Carl yelled at Andy, leaning over, pushing his cup into Andy's face. "Say when, brother!" Andy shouted, lifting the bottle, pouring. Carl did not hold the cup at a forty-five-degree angle. He never did say when. Someone flicked the lights off and on, off and on. Someone, maybe Vince, had a few words to say. Tommy raised his cup to Robert, who stood across the room. They had never really spoken that much in all these years. The sparkling wine foamed over the edge of Carl's cup like a fountain, and the men, several of them, howled.

David, the young Web specialist, left the bathroom and stepped past the pile of cleats at the door. None of the men saw him leave the room. He closed the door behind him quietly, then hung the *Do Not Disturb* sign on the handle. He walked down the hallway, past the surveillance camera, toward the elevator. His regular shoes felt strange and soft, and they made no sound on the carpet. He patted his pockets—phone, keys, wallet, mouthguard. His girlfriend, far away, knew nothing about his night. He pressed the button, and waited. Standing by the elevator doors, he could still hear the voices of the men in Room 324, chanting.

It occurred to David only now, outside the room, divested of his gear, that he could do this again next November with his own group of guys. He would not convene here, of course. He would meet in a better hotel, with a better conference room, a better breakfast. He'd use a projector and a big screen, a podium with A/V controls. He'd get new and better uniforms and equipment. He'd find twenty-one guys, the right kind. Certainly he would need a better field, with bright lights and chalked lines. His uncle was an assistant athletic director at a private high school. David nodded. That field was nice. He imagined wearing the old helmet with the single crossbar, breaking the close huddle, jogging to the line of scrimmage, calling the signals, the colors and numbers. He didn't care about a lottery drum—that thing back there on the bed was ridiculous—but he could make something simple, a box with a small hinged opening on the top or the side. And the thing is, there had to be some kind of lottery system, with meticulous rules so that everything was fair. The same guy couldn't be Theismann every year. Everyone would get a chance.

ACKNOWLEDGMENTS

Lisa Bankoff.
Matt Weiland!
Sam MacLaughlin.
Dave Cole.
Remy Cawley.
Lorin Stein.
Nicole Rudick.
Michael Griffith.

The Sustainable Arts Foundation.
The Taft Research Center, University of Cincinnati.

Alice and Claire.
Jennifer Habel.

Kathy Buckley (1947–2014).
Alice Rightor (1920–2015).

Thank you.